Poachers in the Pingos

ANITA DAHER

ORCA BOOK PUBLISHERS

Text copyright © 2008 Anita Daher

Library and Archives Canada Cataloguing in Publication

Daher, Anita, 1965-
Poachers in the Pingos / written by Anita Daher.

(Orca young readers)
ISBN 978-1-55469-011-4

I. Title. II. Series.

PS8557.A35P62 2008   jC813'.6   C2008-903052-4

First published in the United States, 2008
Library of Congress Control Number: 2008928572

Summary: In this sequel to *Racing for Diamonds*,
Colly and Jaz travel to Tuktoyaktuk and come face-to-face
with a poaching operation involving gyrfalcons.

Orca Book Publishers gratefully acknowledges the support for its publishing programs
provided by the following agencies: the Government of Canada through the Book
Publishing Industry Development Program and the Canada Council for the Arts,
and the Province of British Columbia through the
BC Arts Council and the Book Publishing Tax Credit.

Cover artwork by Glen Bernabe
Author photo by Jeannine Lillie

ORCA BOOK PUBLISHERS
PO Box 5626, STN. B
VICTORIA, BC CANADA
V8R 6S4

ORCA BOOK PUBLISHERS
PO Box 468
CUSTER, WA USA
98240-0468

www.orcabook.com
Printed and bound in Canada.

11 10 09 08 • 4 3 2 1

For Matthew, Rielle, Luke and Thaniel

Acknowledgments

My deepest gratitude to the Winnipeg Arts Council, which kept me in mac and cheese during the writing of this book, to my family and to good friends, writers and information sources: Kelly Hughes, Candace Hughes and Ariel Gordon at Aqua Books; Jamie Bastedo; Captain Conrad Schubert; Dennis Allen; Brad Heath; Terrianne Berens; Rick Shalala; Gerhard (Gary) Albl of Windsurfing Manitoba; and Maureen Pokiak of Ookpik Tours & Adventures Ltd. in Tuktoyaktuk. Thanks also to Marie Campbell, my agent and greatest support, and to my editor Sarah Harvey, publicist Dayle Sutherland and the rest of Team Orca. I appreciate you all so very much.

Thanks also to my farty old hound, Copper, who inspired much of the conversation in this story about "wind."

Chapter One

"You and him got somethin' in common, hey?"

Colly jumped. He'd been watching a raven in a large cage beside the front desk of the Aviary Hotel and Tea House. The cage door was open, and he was wondering if it was supposed to be. He hadn't noticed the man come up behind him.

"What do you mean?" Colly asked, although he was pretty sure he already knew the answer. He just wanted to hear him to say it.

The man was wearing big green gumboots and a bulky sweater. As he moved behind the counter, he spat a glob of grape-smelling bubblegum into a garbage bin. His hair was brown with flecks of gray, and his eyes were small. To Colly, they looked cold, like birds' eyes. He'd never really liked birds. They were something you shot and put in a pot. He'd never thought of them as pets.

"The blue eyes, kid. Are you Metis?"

"No, I'm Dene," Colly said. He was so tired of always having to explain. The Metis were descendants of aboriginal people who had married French, Scots and English settlers. Blue eyes were not unusual if you were Metis. But he was Dene, descended from a long line of First Nations people.

"Really? Guess you're both freaks of nature, then. Not that it's a bad thing." The man erupted in laughter as he began tapping on a computer keyboard, and Colly began a slow boil.

It was true that Dene didn't usually have blue eyes, but in his family it happened every few generations. It wasn't a big deal in Destiny, where he lived. People were used to it. But this was Tuktoyaktuk, a hamlet on the shore of the Arctic Ocean, seven hundred miles northwest of Destiny.

"Oh, come on. Lighten up, kid!" The man leaned over the counter and gave him what was probably meant to be a friendly punch in the arm. "Who wants

Outside, Colly handed Jaz half his sandwich, and they munched as they set off up the long main street toward the harbor. It was like heading for the edge of the world. Tuk sat on a peninsula that was a mostly flat slab of land jutting out like a thumb into the ocean. The slab was actually more like a patch of mud that someone wearing rubber boots had jumped through. There were lakes and marshy bits everywhere. There were also hills and lots of flowers, shrubs and moss, but no trees. Colly knew this kind of northern land without trees was called tundra. They'd passed the last tree just after they'd flown over Inuvik, the next closest town to the south, but still a hundred miles away. There had to be trees somewhere, though. Driftwood looking like bleached dinosaur bones littered the beaches up and down the coast as far as Colly could see. Maybe the wood floated up the Mackenzie River, just like the barges that brought supplies from the south.

"There it is!" Jaz cried.

"What?"

"The caribou!"

Colly squinted, peering toward the distant rocks. "I think you're seeing things."

to be the same as everyone else? That would be pretty boring."

As Colly rubbed his arm, the phrase *Respect your elders* ran through his mind. It was something that had been drummed into his head for as long as he could remember. But sheesh, sometimes it was a pretty difficult thing to do.

Respect was something they talked about a lot in his JCR patrol. JCR was short for Junior Canadian Rangers. There were JCR patrols in communities all across northern Canada. Colly had been a member since he turned twelve and had been made master corporal just before his thirteenth birthday—something that had at first irked Jaz, his fellow JCR. But that was before they'd become friends.

There was a sudden flurry of activity behind him as Jaz entered the foyer. "Come on, Colly, I want to explore!"

They'd arrived in Tuk (which was what most people called Tuktoyaktuk) by airplane that morning for a visit with Colly's Uncle Norbert. "Just a minute," Colly said. "I'm getting something to eat." He handed the unpleasant man some money and accepted a tightly wrapped egg sandwich in return.

"Am not. It's there. Everyone says so!"

Colly's uncle had told him that the name Tuktoyaktuk meant "looks like a caribou" in the Inuvialuit language. It came from a legend about how once upon a time a caribou waded into the water and became petrified. To Colly, looking for a caribou shape in clumps of rocks was kind of like squinting at clouds. You saw what you wanted to see.

When they'd gone as far as they could possibly go, Colly and Jaz kicked off their sneakers and dipped their toes in the ocean.

"It's freezing!" Jaz cried. "It sure doesn't feel like July."

"You're just soft. I dare you to put your whole foot in."

"No way—I dare you to put BOTH your feet in."

"I will if you will." Colly nodded toward a couple of young kids farther down the beach who were running in and out of the water in shorts and long-sleeved T-shirts, splashing each other. They sure weren't soft! He laughed as Jaz made a face and stuck out her tongue at him. It was easy to forget people like the man at the hotel when you were just kicking around with a pal.

Except now he was thinking about him again. Darn.

"What did you think of that creep at the hotel?" Colly asked.

Jaz shrugged. "It's obvious that *you* don't like him." She paused to skip a rock and watch it sink. "Question is, why?"

"He was being a jerk."

"Like how?"

"Did you see that raven with the blue eyes? The guy said we were both freaks of nature."

"That's so mean! Maybe he just didn't think before he opened his mouth. I do that sometimes."

"No kidding!"

Jaz gave him a shove. "I don't know why you're so touchy, anyway. Blue eyes make you special."

Colly sighed. "Yeah, that's what the creep said."

"There. See? He didn't mean to bug you."

"Maybe not."

They left the beach and started walking back up the main road toward the building where the town council took care of all their business. Just after they had arrived that morning, Uncle Norbert had gone out on a patrol, but he had told them that he would be back right after lunch, and that he would meet them there.

They turned at the sound of crunching gravel, and a tall, lean blond man wearing a black scuba-diving suit with yellow stripes sailed past them on a skate-board with a sail.

"That's pretty weird," Colly said.

Jaz shrugged.

As they walked along the gravel road, they passed an old schooner called *Lady of Lourdes* that looked permanently parked on shore. Next to the old ship there was a white wooden church with a green roof and green trim, and a cemetery that looked out over the sea.

"I don't get why you're so touchy, anyway," Jaz said. "Why do you get so mad when people talk about your eyes?"

Colly realized he was gritting his teeth. "I'm not mad!"

"Sound mad to me."

He sighed. "Fine. I'll tell you, but then you have to drop it. "

"I promise," Jaz said.

"I think my family is cursed."

"Did someone come along and put a hex on you or something?" She grinned and waggled her fingers in the air like she was doing some sort of magical spell.

"Stop it, Jaz! I'm not kidding."

She lowered her hands. "Sorry. What do you mean?"

"Blue-eyed boys in our family die young and in terrible accidents."

"That doesn't mean your family is cursed."

He shrugged. "Maybe not, but…" He felt a painful lump in his throat and tried to swallow it. "It happened again. Last month my cousin Junie was fishing back in Fort Chip. A freak storm came up. They figure his boat capsized, and he didn't have his life jacket on."

"He died?"

"Yeah."

"Oh, Colly, that's awful! I'm so sorry," she said, her eyes big and sad. After a moment she frowned. "He had blue eyes?"

"Yeah," he said again, kicking at stones.

Thankfully, Jaz dropped it. Maybe she believed him, and maybe she didn't, but it didn't matter. As long as he didn't have to talk about it.

As they neared the building where they were to meet Colly's uncle, they looked for his beat-up green truck. Seeing it there waiting just outside the wooden front steps, Colly felt a glow spread through him. Uncle Norbert was his dad's adopted brother, and he had always been Colly's favorite. He'd lived with Colly and his family for a while before moving to Tuk, where he had become a member of the Canadian Rangers.

Suddenly the building's front door flew open. "Hi, kids!" Uncle Norbert called, grinning. "Ready for some fun?"

Chapter Two

"I figured you might like to see the pingos Tuktoyaktuk is so famous for," Uncle Norbert said, waving for them to hop into his truck. Two minutes later, they were pulling up to the harbor where half a dozen JCRs were waiting for them.

As a Ranger, Uncle Norbert was one of the leaders of the local JCR patrol. Even though they'd finished their regular meetings for the year, Uncle Norbert figured this was a special occasion and a good reason for a special JCR outing.

"Jaz, Colly, this is Tommy Toner," Uncle Colly said, introducing them to a smiling Inuk boy of about their age.

"Come with me!" Tommy called as he hopped into a waiting boat.

"Go ahead," Uncle Norbert said. "We'll have plenty of time to visit later on."

As Colly stepped into Tommy's boat he felt a tightness in his belly, and he tried to will it away. As soon as he fastened his bright orange life jacket, it eased up. Enough that he could ignore it, anyway. He looked back toward the beach as they pulled away and spotted the blond man they'd seen earlier on the winged skateboard. He was pulling open the door of a shed and taking out a windsurfing board.

"So what's with that guy and his weird skateboard?" Colly asked Tommy.

"That's the wind researcher the town hired," Tommy said. He looked comfortable steering the boat, as if he'd spent most of his life on the water. Probably he had. Besides the ocean, there were a couple of hundred lakes on the Tuktoyaktuk Peninsula. "The skateboard is just how he gets around—on land, anyway."

"Why does the town need a wind researcher?"

"They want to build a wind farm."

Jaz turned to them from the front of the speedboat, eyes wide, short red curls bobbing. "Is this town called Crazyville?" she asked. "Why would anyone want to grow wind?"

Colly and Tommy burst out laughing. "It's okay, Jaz," Colly said. "You're much younger than us, so we don't expect you to know about wind farms."

Jaz stuck out her tongue. "I'm only one year and seven months younger than you are, Colly Bruno, and you'd better tell me, or I'll push you into the Arctic Ocean!"

"I'm just teasing you, Jaz!" Colly said. "But technically, around here it's the Beaufort Sea."

"Whatever!"

"So is this how Destiny Patrol settles their arguments?" Tommy joked. "A wind farm captures the power from wind and makes electricity people can use in their houses."

"Anyone can see it's windy," Colly said, zipping his jacket a little higher up his neck. "Why do they need a researcher?"

Tommy just shrugged and smiled. Colly noticed that Tommy smiled a lot. It made Colly want to smile back.

An old man in a checked jacket and a flat cap waved from a bench facing the harbor as Tommy kicked the motor into full speed. Colly gasped as his breath was ripped away, and the wind hit him full in the face.

It was early summer, but there was still an icy bite in the air. It was something he could feel and taste. It was probably because the wind was from the north-west. It was always colder coming from that direction. He sunk his chin into his collar and ran his tongue over his teeth to warm them.

"There they are!" Jaz called, squinching up her face. "They don't really look like zits."

"What are you talking about?" Tommy asked.

Colly rolled his eyes. "She thought they looked like pimples on the map we printed off the Internet." From the boat they could see just two pingos, though he knew there were about one thousand four hundred of them of all different sizes on the Tuk peninsula. "To me they look like bubbles in a pot of porridge," he said. The one they were heading for looked like a bubble that had burst at the top, but still otherwise held its bubble shape.

"Yeah! Green and brown porridge," Jaz added.

Tommy just laughed. "Only on the outside. Pingos are made of ice, you know. This one is more than a thousand years old and still growing."

Colly and Jaz had read about the pingos after Uncle Norbert invited them to visit. They'd learned that Tuktoyaktuk was home to the Pingo National Landmark, which wasn't quite a national park, but close enough. The ice Tommy mentioned was actually called permafrost—permanent frost—because it never went away. Pingos were created when underground water pressure pushed the permafrost up into hills— kind of like miniature volcanoes, but without the lava. They were all different sizes. Some were only as big as a house, and others were much bigger. The Ibyuk Pingo, closest to Tuk, was as tall as a sixteen-story office building. Many of the pingos were surrounded by water, which made getting to them by boat much easier than finding a way over the tundra. "Why are they called pingos?" Jaz asked. "It's a funny name."

"The name means 'small hill' in my language," Tommy said.

"What language is that?"

Tommy grinned. "Inuvialuktun."

The boats pushed up onto the stony shore, and ten JCRs in green sweatshirts with red logos and matching green ball caps peeled off their life jackets and scrambled out. Uncle Norbert was right behind them in a red Ranger sweatshirt with a green logo.

"Enjoy your ride?" he asked Colly.

"Yeah, Tommy's a good driver."

"Ahh…I was going easy on you," Tommy said. "I don't know yet if you scare easy."

Jaz burst out laughing. Colly shot her a look, even though he could understand why she thought it was funny. Maybe Tommy had forgotten about Colly and Jaz's run-in with Russian diamond smugglers a few months earlier. He had to know about it, as he too had been racing in the sled-dog derby along with all the other JCR patrols in the Northwest Territories.

But Jaz shouldn't be laughing about being scared on a boat. Not after what Colly had told her about his cousin Junie.

"I think they can handle themselves, Tommy," Uncle Norbert said.

Another boy bumped Tommy with his shoulder. "At least Tommy stayed on this side of the water."

Colly looked at his uncle. Did everyone know about Junie? As if reading his mind, Uncle Norbert shook his head and squeezed Colly's shoulder.

Tommy just waved his hand as if swatting away a fly. "I sink my boat just once, and no one lets me live it down!" The others giggled. Obviously this was a ribbing Tommy was used to. It had nothing to do with Junie.

"It gets pretty windy around here," Uncle Norbert said, "and Tommy here swamped his boat as he was coming in from fishing one day."

"I was ten feet from the dock," Tommy said. "Stupid!"

"Not stupid at all," Uncle Norbert said. "Just goes to show you that you have to always be watchful."

"*Vigilans*!" one of the girls called out.

"That's right, Jenny."

Colly and all the other JCRs knew that *Vigilans* was the motto of the Canadian Rangers. It was a Latin word that meant "the watchers." Canadian Rangers were the "eyes and ears" across the North, making sure all was as it should be.

Jaz was gazing up the side of the pingo. "Can we go, Sergeant Norbert?"

"Sure! Just make sure you are respectful of the vegetation. It serves as a protective layer between the sun, and the ice inside the pingo."

"Kick the Earth, kill a pingo?" she asked.

"Something like that," Sergeant Norbert said, smiling. "If the sun starts melting the ice, the pingo will collapse."

Chapter Three

Colly and Jaz meandered up the side of the pingo, exploring carefully so as not to disturb any of the grasses or moss. The higher they climbed, the more spectacular the view became. On the ocean side the white-flecked gray water went on and on until it met the cloud-pocked sky. Turning toward Tuktoyaktuk, Colly drank in the sight of the gently rolling marsh and the tundra dotted with hummocks. The land was bursting with color! He saw tiny white mountain avens, their flower faces following the sun; the heavy heads of orange Arctic poppies balanced on spindly stocks. He looked up and felt dizzy. The sky was so big and the land was so open, it was kind of overwhelming.

"Come on!" Jaz called as she raced back down the side of the pingo toward the beach, where the other JCRs were gathering for lunch.

Colly wasn't quite ready to follow. This place was so special. He closed his eyes and imagined a hunter looking out over the land, watching for caribou.

He wanted that to be him. He loved the land, just as his ancestors had. Loved camping, hunting, fishing—all of it. He loved being a JCR, and he was good at it. One day he wanted to be a Ranger, like Uncle Norbert.

At least, that was what he'd always thought.

Lately though, everything had gone sour. Whenever his dad asked him if he wanted to go hunting or fishing, it was never a good time. At least, that was what he told his dad. Really, that wasn't it.

It was Junie.

Junie was his dad's oldest sister's son, five years older than Colly, with blue eyes, just like him. He had so many good memories of Junie from back when they had all still lived in Fort Chip: Junie giving him an airplane ride when he was five; Junie helping make an awesome hairy Sasquatch costume when he was seven; Junie taking him out to count birds very early one summer morning when he was nine.

The summer they went bird counting was the summer Colly and his family moved to Destiny. It was the last time he'd seen Junie.

But they kept in touch. Sort of. Colly knew from what his dad told him that when Junie finished high school, he wanted to study to be a park ranger. That would have been this year.

Instead, Junie had drowned.

Why hadn't he worn his life jacket? Junie knew better. He knew ALL about living and surviving outdoors, and he had taught Colly so much before Colly moved to Destiny. He'd taught him things his father never could. Colly's father was an accountant who spent most of his time indoors. He just didn't *get* the outdoors.

But Junie was a born outdoorsman. Forgetting about his life jacket or choosing not to wear it just didn't make sense.

The only thing that made sense was a curse. Especially when he started putting the pieces together. Blue-eyed boys just didn't have good luck in his family.

Colly sighed, opened his eyes and looked toward the town. It was only a few miles away, though the water-pocked bog made a boat ride over the ocean much easier than a hike. Still, he could clearly see the blue, green and white buildings. He could even see a four-wheel quad bike pass a blue truck traveling south down the main street. He watched the quad as it headed north to the harbor, then he let his gaze fall onto the bay. There was something out of place. A wing—or rather, a sail. It was that wind researcher guy, except now, instead of windsurfing over land on a skateboard, he was doing it on the water. Another flutter caught his attention. Two wings—a black bird was swooping around the windsurfer's head. A raven? It had to be. But it was kind of weird that it was sticking to the windsurfer like that. Maybe the guy had a cheeseburger tied around his neck.

His stomach growled, and he trotted down the trail toward the others.

"Glad you decided to join us," Uncle Norbert said. His eyes crinkled as he smiled and handed Colly a plate of food. Colly tore into it with gusto—warm bannock, fresh-baked over a fire, dried whitefish, and white squares of something he didn't recognize. He held one up and sniffed.

"It's muktuk," Tommy said. "Beluga whale skin and blubber."

Colly frowned and endured a poke in the ribs from Jaz. "It's good, try it!" she said.

He bit into it. It tasted a little like chicken and a little like scrambled eggs...but chewier. "Not bad," he agreed as he chewed and swallowed. It was all delicious, especially the chocolate chip cookies.

A sudden gust of wind scattered bits and pieces of leftover lunch, sending the JCRs laughing and scrambling after them. Afterward, Uncle Norbert gathered them around. "Supposing there was a real bad storm and all your boats were swept out to sea..."

"Like that would happen!" one girl scoffed.

"Maybe to Tommy," a boy said, elbowing Tommy.

"Hey!" Tommy said, but Colly could see he wasn't bothered.

"Well, *if* it happened," Uncle Norbert continued, "and you had no other way of getting home, do you know the ground-to-air signals that let a search plane know your status?"

Most of the JCRs shook their heads. Colly thought he might have heard about this before, but he wasn't sure, so he stayed silent. He watched as Uncle Norbert scratched one symbol after another into the mud and explained what each meant.

"Use something that can be easily seen by air. On mud like this, use white stones. As many as you can find."

"If there was a storm, would the airplanes still fly?"

"Depends on the airplane," Jaz said. "My dad told me that—he's a pilot."

"Do you know how to fly too?"

"Not yet, but maybe someday." She tilted her head to the side. "Actually, I do know some things. Last summer my sort-of-cousin Kaylee and I learned a lot about flying, and how to land and take off facing into the wind."

Colly leaned close to his friend. "Jaz, we're not here to learn about flying."

Uncle Norbert laughed. "That's okay, Colly. It's all good information. Maybe we should have a field trip to the airport one day. Any more questions about the ground-to-air symbols?"

"Just one," Jaz said. "How big do they have to be?"

"As big as you can possibly make them, Jaz. The recommended size is forty feet long and ten feet wide."

"Whoa!" Jaz's eyes were wide.

"Don't worry, little mouse," Tommy said, grinning. "We won't leave you stranded."

"That's right," Uncle Norbert said. "But maybe some of you will leave some others in the dust. Who's up for a three-legged race?"

There were cheers as the JCRs paired off and tied their legs together. Taller kids were paired with shorter ones, just to make things more awkward than they already were.

"Ready?" Uncle Norbert asked, his arm raised high above his head. "One…two…three…go!"

Five teams of JCRs took off down the stony beach toward the marker—a piece of driftwood leaning against a mud ridge like a giant white chicken bone. Soon everyone was giggling as they tried to stay upright and get ahead. Colly, the tallest of the bunch, was paired with Tommy, the shortest. Suddenly, Colly stopped.

"What the—?" Tommy cried, falling forward.

"Sorry," Colly said, "but look! In those tall weeds."

He pointed at five dead birds—white, with tiny black flecks. Falcons.

"Oh great," Tommy groaned. "The poacher strikes again."

Chapter Four

"A poacher? How can you tell?" Colly asked. "Maybe they died naturally."

Catching up with them, Uncle Norbert shook his head. "All together like this, neatly stacked? No, this was deliberate."

The other JCRs abandoned the race and gathered round.

"But why?" Jaz asked.

"We haven't figured that out yet, Jaz. But I promise you—we will!"

"What kind of birds are they?"

"Gyrfalcons," Tommy said.

"Jar falcons?" Jaz repeated.

Tommy smiled. "Almost. It rhymes with 'burr.'"

She tried again. "Burr-falcons, jurr-falcons."

"That's right!" He looked at the birds again. "It's weird that they're white, though. Mostly you see gray ones around here."

The ground looked like it had been trampled, but Colly couldn't tell by what. He spotted a long dark feather on the ground and picked it up. It was probably from a raven, which wasn't at all unusual. "Don't touch anything," Uncle Norbert said.

"I thought it might be a clue," Colly said, dropping the feather where he had found it.

"We get lots of people passing through Tuk," Uncle Norbert said. "Hunters, people from the military's North Warning Site, visiting government workers. It could be anyone." He frowned. "This is the third bunch of dead gyrfalcons we've found."

"And that's not all," Tommy said. "There was a musk ox, which is weird because there aren't any musk ox herds around here. Lots of caribou—but no musk ox."

"Maybe it just got lost," Jaz said.

"Maybe," Tommy said, "except someone took its horns."

"Was it a hunter?" Jaz asked.

Colly shook his head. "Couldn't be. No hunter would waste the meat like that."

Uncle Norbert slapped his thighs and stood. "Come on, gang. Time to call it a day!"

He looked grim as they gathered their things from the beach and climbed back into their boats. Before long they were back in the Tuktoyaktuk harbor and on the dock. The old man on the bench waved them in.

"Hi, Grandfather!" Tommy called, then turned to Colly and Jaz. "Come on, I'll introduce you."

Tommy's grandfather helped them tie the boat and offered each of them a hand onto the dock. "You can call me Grandfather too, okay?" he said. "Have you been out to see the pingos?"

"Yeah, they're pretty cool!" Jaz cried.

Grandfather nodded. "When I was a boy, we dug into one of the pingos and used it as a meat freezer."

"Really?" Colly asked, pulling out his map. "Which one?"

Grandfather ran his hand over the paper, his brow creased. "It's not on this map," he said. "Close, though." He tapped the edge of it. "Somewhere over here."

"Is it still a meat freezer?" Jaz asked.

"The last time I looked, a grizzly bear was using it for a den, but that was a long time ago." He looked wistful. "I'd like to look again."

"If you remember where it is, maybe I can go there with you," Tommy said.

Grandfather smiled, his eyes twinkling. "That would be nice, Tommy. Maybe you can drive my boat."

Colly laughed. "I hear he needs the practice."

"Hey!"

Once the boats were moored, the other JCRs scattered. Uncle Norbert said he had to report the dead gyrfalcons; he would find Jaz and Colly later. As he hopped into his truck and drove off, Colly saw the windsurfer tucking his water equipment back into the shed and pulling out his strange skateboard.

"Hey, Philip!" Tommy called. "I want you to meet my friends, Jaz and Colly."

"Philip Slaytor," the man said as they arrived at the shed. "Nice to meet you."

From a distance, Colly had thought he'd been looking at some sort of beach bum surfer dude like he'd seen on TV, but up close he could see that the man was older than he expected. He had weathered leathery skin and creases around his eyes, but he was really fit-looking. Maybe it was because of the windsurfing.

"How was the water today?" Tommy asked.

"Terrific! The wind was about as perfect as it can get. I heard it's supposed to get pretty strong later, so I wanted to get some surfing in now."

"I told them what you're doing," Tommy said. "They want to know more about the wind farm."

"Yeah, about that," Jaz said. "How do you catch wind?"

"Well…you know how to pass wind, right?"

Tommy snorted, Jaz grinned and Colly rolled his eyes.

"Just kidding—I only wanted to make sure you were listening," Philip said. "We catch wind by putting up wind turbines, and…"

"What are those?" Jaz asked.

"Have you seen pictures of windmills?"

"Yeah."

"That's what they are, except ours are much more modern and efficient. The wind turns the blades and creates energy. That energy is captured with a generator. The generator converts the energy to electricity, and there you go. A place with lots of wind turbines is called a wind farm. Make sense?"

"Sure! But maybe using people wind to make energy would be a good idea too."

Philip laughed. "It'll take a better wind researcher than me to figure that one out, Jaz. Maybe someday, huh? I know of some scientists who are already doing great things with cow farts."

Colly grinned, no longer annoyed with Jaz's references to pimples and wind. Jaz was Jaz, and no one would make her change. That was one of the things he liked about her.

Philip was easy to like too. He seemed pretty comfortable in his own skin, which right now was a wet suit. "When I was on the pingo, I saw you wind-surfing," Colly said. "It looked like fun."

"Have you ever tried it?" Philip asked.

"No."

"Would you like to?"

Colly hesitated.

"Of course he would!" Jaz cried. "Me too!"

Philip laughed. "Here, let me give you a quick lesson."

"But we don't have wet suits…or life jackets."

"No worries. We'll start with a land lesson. Sound good?"

Colly grinned. "Sure."

Standing on the board, hanging onto the sail, Philip leaned one way and then another, showing them the basic crosswind stance, as well as how to turn upwind and downwind. As Colly took his turn on the board, he felt the wind catch the sail with such strength, he thought he might start moving over the sand toward the water. The wind was getting too strong, and so the lesson came to an end.

"What do you think?" Philip asked Colly.

"No sweat."

"Colly is always good at stuff," Jaz said. "I bet he could do it on water."

"I'm sure he could. Maybe we can give it a try after the wind dies down a bit. "

"Sure," Colly said, but his stomach gave a strange twist as he said it. "As long as we have life jackets."

Philip stowed his windsurfer and brought out his landsurfer.

"That's a pretty weird board," Colly said.

"Not where I come from."

"Where is that?" Jaz asked.

"He's from Hollywood!" Tommy said.

"Not quite," Philip said, grinning. "But I am from southern California."

"That's a long way," Colly said. "How did you get this job?"

"I grew up in the same small town as a guy who runs the Aviary Hotel. Hadn't seen him since I was ten or twelve, but I ran into him last summer at a convention in Denver, Colorado. He told me that Tuk was thinking about getting a wind farm, so I got in touch with the town council."

"Have you been here all winter?"

"Nope—just a few months. I've been staying at the hotel."

Tommy opened his mouth as if he had something to add, but his attention suddenly turned to something behind Colly. His eyes grew wide. As Colly spun around, he was met by a screech not unlike someone scratching fingernails over a blackboard…if they had fingernails made of steel.

Chapter Five

"It's just a raven!" Colly said, ignoring the thump-thump of his heart.

But it wasn't like other ravens. It had blue eyes, like the one he'd seen at the hotel. Maybe it was the same one. After all, how many blue-eyed ravens could there be?

Wings spread, it walked toward them. It screeched again, and Colly covered his ears.

"I hate that bird," Tommy growled.

It lowered its wings and cocked its head to one side as if listening.

"Watch out, it likes to chew on things," Tommy said.

"Like what?" Jaz asked.

"Oh you know, toys, bikes…people."

"Oh there you are, Beastie," a man said, coming around the shed toward them. "Were you missing your friend?"

Colly frowned. It was the rude man from the hotel.

The bird hopped up on Philip's shoulder, and extended his beak as if looking for a kiss. "We've got to stop meeting like this," Philip said, laughing and stroking the bird's head.

"Is that some sort of a trick raven?" Colly asked.

"Not quite. But he's been around people for quite some time," Philip said. "I think he has a crush on me."

The other man turned to Jaz and Colly. "Didn't I see you kids earlier?"

Colly gritted his teeth. "Yes, sir," he said. "I bought a sandwich from you."

The man snapped his fingers. "Of course. You and Beastie here both have blue eyes." He smiled the same unpleasant smile Colly had seen earlier. Then he unwrapped a sucker and popped it in his mouth.

Cherry. Colly could smell it from three feet away.

"This is the old friend I was telling you about," Philip said. "Jaz, Colly, meet Harvey Chiapot."

Harvey nodded and winked. "Philip has been staying with me for a few months."

"So we heard," Colly mumbled.

"My boy Beastie here took a liking to him and follows him sometimes."

"Is it safe for him to fly around loose like that, Mr. Chiapot?" Jaz asked.

"Call me Harvey," he said. "And yeah, Beastie was born in the wild and still is wild, far as I'm concerned."

"But he lives in a cage," Colly said.

"But the door is always open," Harvey said, waggling his finger at him. "Beastie goes where he wants. Even if he doesn't hang out much with his wild brothers and sisters anymore, I bet he could still hold his own."

"Against some things, maybe," Philip said.

"Anything too big, he'll just fly home."

"What about falcons?" Tommy asked. "A gyrfalcon would take him out pretty quick."

Instead of answering, Harvey looked at Tommy and frowned as if remembering something. "I saw your fearless leader blazing down the road a few minutes ago. What's up?"

"You mean Sergeant Norbert?" Tommy asked. "We found another bunch of dead gyrfalcons. We think poachers got them."

"Is that right?" Harvey asked, but it didn't really sound like a question. His eyes had a faraway look as he smacked his cherry sucker. "That sergeant of yours sure is eager to get the job done."

Even though the words sounded normal, Colly got the feeling Harvey was making fun of his uncle. He squeezed his hands into fists, growling inside his head. Jaz exchanged a quick glance with him. "Ah, Mr. Chiapot," she said.

"Call me Harvey. I insist!"

"Okay," Jaz said, but she looked doubtful. "I just wanted to tell you that Sergeant Norbert is Colly's uncle."

"That's nice," he said. He extended an arm for Beastie and waited as the bird transferred itself from Philip's shoulder to his own. "I've got to get back to the Aviary," he said. "You kids be good and come by later for some pie!"

"That guy bugs me," Colly muttered as Harvey Chiapot and Beastie disappeared around the corner of a house.

"Harvey?" Philip asked. "He's okay. A bit rough around the edges, maybe, but harmless. Some people just aren't very good at communicating."

"He sure likes birds," Jaz said.

Philip nodded. "And they like him. If Harvey had a real aviary instead of just a hotel named for one, I think he would be the happiest guy on earth."

"Has he *always* liked birds?" Colly asked.

"Even when we were kids," Philip said. "But the North has a lot more interesting birds than back home—like those gyrfalcons you were talking about. I bet he'd love to have one of those in his cage."

"It's against the law to keep wild birds," Tommy said. "I'm not even sure he's supposed to keep Beastie."

"Yeah, but like he said, Beastie can come and go whenever he wants." Philip winked and shut the door to his shed. "Well, I'd best get back to wind-catching."

"Better than wind-passing," Jaz said, grinning. Colly groaned.

"You bet—see you later!"

As Philip caught a breeze and scooted up the road on his landsurfer, Jaz, Tommy and Colly wandered, kicking at stones. Gulls were flying over the harbor, reminding Colly of something. "When I was on the pingo, I saw a raven flying around Philip," he said. "Do you think it was Beastie?"

"Probably," Tommy said. "Beastie follows him around like some kind of puppy dog."

"So he really does have a crush on him?"

"I don't know," Tommy said, laughing.

They meandered through town, following a side road past Mangilaluk School, where a scattering of young children were playing tag. As they walked, they talked about their adventure at the pingo and what they'd found.

"I don't get it," Jaz said. "Why would poachers want to kill gyrfalcons?"

Tommy shrugged. "Why does a poacher want to kill anything?" he asked.

"Food or money," Colly said.

Jaz frowned. "It doesn't look like they wanted the food."

"So it must be money," Tommy said. "But it's strange that they left them behind."

"Maybe they planned to come back for them," Colly said. "It's also strange that it only started a few months ago. Have there been any suspicious-looking people in town?"

Tommy thought. "Not really. Any hunters that come up from the south go with outfitters, and there's no way an outfitter would let them waste the meat like they did with the musk ox."

A little farther down the road they came to a small white wooden shack with a lock on it.

"What's in there?" Colly asked.

"Is it where they keep poachers?" Jaz asked.

Colly rolled his eyes, but Tommy only laughed. "You guys are funny! It's our icehouse—an underground freezer for the whole community. Want to see?"

"Sure!"

"Wait here. I'll get the key!"

Colly was about to ask Tommy where he lived, but a sound caught his attention. A siren was sounding from somewhere, but the wind made it sound far off, coming to them only in gusts. Tommy and Jaz heard it too. They turned toward the sound and saw people running toward the harbor. Three trucks, including Uncle Norbert's, spun by, kicking up gravel.

"What the heck is going on?" Colly asked.

Chapter Six

Colly, Tommy and Jaz sprinted back up the street to the harbor, where they found Uncle Norbert sending people in different directions. "It's an emergency drill," he said, peering across white-capped waves in the harbor. "We received what sounded like a distress call, but it cut off right away."

"A drill?" Jaz asked.

"It's a test of the town's emergency response team," Tommy said. "We knew it was coming, but we didn't know when."

"Can we help?" Colly asked.

Uncle Norbert shook his head. "We all have roles already assigned, Colly. Tommy will take you to Sherry at Radio Dispatch. She's expecting you. It'll be interesting for you to listen in."

They ran down the road, and soon they were standing on the doorstep of an official-looking green building with a red roof and blue trim. Tommy shouted an introduction to someone inside, said he would see them later and took off.

"I feel like we should be doing something," Jaz said.

Colly shrugged. "Me too, but we'd probably just get in the way." He poked his head inside. "Hello?"

"Come on in here, kids!" a woman called. They could hear static from a radio coming from one of the rooms off the kitchen.

They followed the sounds until they found a big woman with long black hair gathered in a thick ponytail speaking into a handheld microphone. She held a finger up for them to wait. "Operation Ping-Pong is in effect," she said. "Repeat. Operation Ping-Pong is in effect."

She turned to them, eyes bright. "I'm Sherry. There's juice in the fridge, kids. Make yourself at home!"

"Why is it called 'Operation Ping-Pong'?" Jaz asked.

Sherry shrugged. "Information is given to us on a 'need to know' basis," she said. "Right now all we need to know is that Bert and Edna didn't come back from fishing, and that there was a short distress signal."

"Who are Bert and Edna?"

"Someone's made-up auntie and uncle," Sherry said, winking.

"So what happens now?" Colly asked.

"The RCMP is coordinating a search team. I imagine after that there will be a rescue!"

There was another burst of static mixed with garbled words. Sherry turned back to the radio and spoke into the microphone. "Roger that," she said, writing something else in her notebook.

Peering over her shoulder, Colly could see that she was keeping track of groups of searchers and where they were looking. Colly scanned the names, but only recognized Uncle Norbert's and some of the JCR's.

"Should we bring you a cup of coffee or something?" Jaz asked.

Sherry shook her head. "No…just relax. I'll call you if I need you, okay?"

Colly followed Jaz into the kitchen. She pointed to the refrigerator. "Want some juice?"

He shook his head. "I'm not thirsty."

"Me neither. Kind of boring just waiting around while everyone is having fun."

Colly moved toward a wall with a row of clipboards hanging off nails. He picked one up and flipped the pages.

"You shouldn't touch that," Jaz said.

Colly's lips twitched. "You're starting to sound like me, Jaz. Don't worry. If it was private it wouldn't be hanging out here in plain view." He stared at it for a moment, and then handed the clipboard to Jaz. "This looks like a schedule for all the tugboats that move barges in and out of the harbor."

"So?"

Colly shrugged. "So nothing. I was just looking."

Jaz looked at it closely. "Doesn't look like there's anyone out there right now. Think it's too windy?"

"Not for a tug. Just no one scheduled, I guess."

"Not until later. It's pretty interesting though. Look at this. One tugboat pulls all the supply barges up the Mackenzie River to Tuk. When it gets here, the barges are all separated, and a bunch of other tugboats take them to communities all up and down the coast."

"Not all of them," Colly said, tapping the page. "This tug has a departure point and a destination right here in Tuk. I wonder where it goes?"

"Maybe it's a spy boat!"

Colly laughed. "And maybe you've been watching too many movies. What would it be spying on up here? It's more likely just going out to someone's fishing camp."

"Or maybe it's meeting a ship—some big ocean liner or something," Jaz offered. She peered at the clipboard. "The tug's called the *R & C Stampe Collector*. That's a funny name. 'Stamp' is spelled wrong."

"It's probably named after someone—lots of boats are. Look, it leaves in a few hours."

"Think it'll still go? Everyone is pretty busy with Operation Ping-Pong."

Colly shrugged. "I can't see it waiting because of a fake emergency."

"I wonder what the tug will be delivering. I mean, I can see taking supplies to the communities, but what would it bring to a ship?"

Colly rolled his eyes. "There is no ship, Jaz…" He was about to tell her to give her head a shake, but an idea had begun tap-tapping inside his own skull. "Wait. Maybe you're on to something."

Jazz ran to the window and looked outside. "Are pigs suddenly flying?" She turned to him. "Because if you think I'm right about something—even though I probably am—the world must be turning upside down."

Colly sucked in his bottom lip, thinking. "People are starting all kinds of businesses. It's possible that not all of them are legal. Maybe someone is sending out the gyrfalcons on a ship. It might be the poacher!"

Jaz made a face. "Don't you think someone would have noticed a bunch of dead gyrfalcons?"

"Maybe the birds weren't meant to be dead. Maybe they were captured and some died."

"What about the dead musk ox and its missing horns? That's part of this too."

"There was only one dead musk ox, compared to three bunches of dead gyrfalcons."

"So?"

"Well…" Colly frowned. "Maybe the poacher panicked when the dead gyrfalcons were found."

"And left the dead musk ox just to confuse things?"

He tapped the pencil a little harder, then flipped it on its end and smacked the eraser side onto the table, like an exclamation point.

"It's probably Harvey Chiapot."

"You're just saying that because you don't like him."

"Not liking him has nothing to do with it, Jaz. Philip said that Harvey is really into birds, and always has been. If anyone is after falcons around here, it's probably him."

"There's no proof of that."

He stood and began pacing. For some reason walking always made his brain work better. He stopped and smiled at her. "Maybe there is. Remember the raven feather I found by the dead birds? It could be from Beastie."

Jaz frowned. "That's not for-sure evidence, Colly. It might not have been from Beastie."

"For crying out loud, Jaz, just go with it, okay? It's not like we have anything better to do. Let's figure this out."

She shrugged. "Fine. Let's say the raven feather is from Beastie, and that Harvey is trying to smuggle out gyrfalcons. You think he's taking them to a ship using the tugboat?"

"If he is, first he'll need to pick them up from wherever he has them stashed," Colly said.

"I noticed some sheds behind his hotel."

Colly shook his head. "There's no way Harvey would keep them in town."

"Why not?"

"Keeping wild birds is against the law, remember? He wouldn't want anyone to see."

"So…the tug is going to pick up gyrfalcons from some hiding place and then bring them to a ship?"

Colly shrugged. "Maybe, maybe not. It's just an idea."

"You're right, Colly. It makes total sense! But…how can we prove it?"

Colly stood. "Before we prove anything, we have to find out if we're right. Let's go take a look at that tug."

Chapter Seven

"Good idea!" Jaz cried, jumping to her feet. "But... practically everyone is busy with Operation Ping-Pong. What if we see something?"

"We'll wait and tell my uncle. The tug isn't scheduled to leave for two hours. I'm sure the fake emergency will be finished by then."

Jaz nodded slowly. "Do you think Sherry will mind us leaving?"

"Let's ask."

Colly poked his head back in the radio room. Sherry was talking and listening and talking again. Colly waited until she noticed him.

"How's it going?" he asked.

Sherry grinned and gave him a thumbs-up. "Stage two. Bert and Edna are down the coast clinging to the face of what used to be a pingo." She stopped and cackled as if this was the best kind of fun. "As soon as the wind dies down we'll get a boat to them."

"When is that going to be?"

"Soon, if the forecast is right."

"Do you need us for anything?"

Sherry smiled. "No, I'm fine. If you want to do something else, you should go ahead."

Colly turned to leave, but stopped when he saw her pick up her notebook. "Sherry, I noticed Harvey Chiapot and Philip Slaytor weren't on the list of searchers. Is it because they're not from here?"

"Nah! Everyone was invited. I'm not sure what Philip's up to, but I think Harvey is giving out cookies to the searchers."

Or maybe he's getting ready to load gyrfalcons onto a tugboat, Colly thought as they hurried to the harbor. Maybe Harvey had fooled everyone else with his cookies and his pie, but not him. At the water's edge they made their way to the commercial dock, where they found the *R & C Stampe Collector* moored in front of the barge it was getting ready to tow. The tug was gray and had tires hanging over the sides all the way around, forming a giant rubber bumper. On top it had one yellow cab sitting on top of a slightly wider cabin, like a two-layer cake. Having lived all his life next to boats and water, Colly knew the top one was called the wheelhouse. That's where all the controls were. The bottom one was probably where the kitchen was—except that on boats it was called a galley—and maybe a bathroom and rest area. Behind the tug, the barge was loaded with crates and plastic-wrapped cardboard boxes of various sizes. There was also one large wooden box, big enough to hold a large deep-freeze or maybe a couple of snowmobiles. On the side of the box there was a large hatch, hinged on one side like a door.

Colly and Jaz ducked behind the corner of a building and watched. Everything looked normal. Boring, even. Once in a while a seagull flew overhead, or a crew member walked across the deck of the *Stampe Collector*, climbed the ladder and then disappeared into the wheelhouse.

Time tick-tick-ticked away, and soon twenty minutes had passed without a sign that the tugboat crew was up to no good. Colly stood. "Wait here," he said.

"Where are you going?"

"If there's any proof of bird smuggling on that barge, it's not going to be in plain sight. I'm going to take a closer look."

"You can't! What if they catch you?"

"I'll be careful," Colly assured her. "Besides, if someone does catch me, I'll just play dumb and say I'm looking for my uncle."

"It'd be better if you didn't get caught."

"No kidding!" He turned back to the barge. "There's space in between some of those stacked boxes. If someone comes, I can hide."

Jaz snorted. "As if! No way you'd fit."

"Guess I'll just have to take my chances."

Jaz grabbed his arm. "Wait. No way *you* would fit, but for me it'd be no sweat."

Colly shook his head and stepped toward the barge. "I can't let you do this, Jaz. Just wait here, and watch out for me."

"Stop it!"

The fury in Jaz's voice made him pause and look at her. Her eyes were flashing, and her skin was flushed.

"Why do you always do this?" she said. "You always make like you're some big hero and that I need looking after."

"What? No...I didn't mean that, Jaz."

"Well, what did you mean? Just because you out-rank me in JCRs doesn't mean you always have to be the one to do everything."

"I don't."

"Yes, you do, Colly. At least you try to. You can't control everything all the time."

For a moment, he said nothing. "Is that what I do?" he finally asked.

Jaz nodded. "Think about it, Colly. A small person has a better chance of poking around on that barge without getting caught. I'm a small person—at least, smaller than you. I should do it. You don't always have to prove you're the best!"

He felt like he'd been punched in the stomach. It wasn't that he thought he was the best...he just thought...actually, he wasn't sure what he thought. "Was I being a jerk?"

He saw Jaz's shoulders relax a little. "Not a jerk, exactly. But you are a little bossy, sometimes."

"Like you're not bossy?"

She grinned and gave him a shove. "Just watch out for me, okay?"

He looked at the boxes again. "Fine. But I'm going with you partway." He pointed to an empty, smashed-up crate abandoned halfway down the dock, next to the barge and close to the tug. "I'll watch from there."

They edged along the side of the shed, and then dashed across the dock to the crate. It wasn't perfect cover, but it was better than nothing.

"Just yell if you see something," Jaz said.

Colly thought for a moment, and then he pulled a red whistle from his pocket. "Even better—I'll use my JCR whistle."

Jaz grinned. "That'll work. Blow that and you'll have the whole Tuk Patrol down here!" The whistle was supposed to be a sort of 911 for the North, to be used in emergencies or if you became lost.

Just as Jaz was about to launch herself over the edge of the barge, Colly spotted movement and grabbed her shoulder. On the tug, a burly man in potato-colored coveralls and a green windbreaker hurried along the deck, and then he disappeared around the side.

When Colly felt pretty sure the man wasn't returning, he nodded at Jaz.

"Relax," she whispered. "This is no big deal." With a wink, she climbed onto the barge and began creeping along the edge of the boxes. After a moment, he couldn't see her anymore.

Where had she gone? It was like he blinked, and she disappeared.

Then he saw her—squeezing out from between two boxes.

She'd been right. No way would Colly have been able to climb through that small space. He kept his eye on the tug, watching for the man in coveralls as Jaz made her way back to him. But instead of jumping onto the dock, she crouched at the edge of the barge.

"It's pretty cool in there!" she whisper-shouted. "Like a whole network of secret passageways…except I know they're not, really. Just piled-up boxes with spaces in between."

"Did you find anything?"

"That big crate at the front might have cages in it, but it's going to take a bit more time for me to find out. I just wanted to let you know."

He looked at the crate. "There's no point," he said. "Looks like it's got a padlock on it."

"I know, but crawling through the passages, I think I saw a crack along an inside edge. I can get closer to look, but I have to climb a bit."

Colly glanced at the tug. All was quiet. "Okay," he said. "But go fast!"

"No problem," she said as she dashed back to the opening and disappeared.

He glanced back at the tug. A man came out on deck and wandered to where the barge was secured, as if checking something. Colly held his breath, hoping the man wouldn't look his way and see him. He also hoped there was no trip alarm on the barge, and that Jaz hadn't set it off.

The man appeared satisfied and moved off.

Colly gave his head a shake and smiled to himself. Trip alarm? He was starting to think like Jaz.

The door opened again, and another man joined the first. The two of them stood, watching something on the far side of the tug, beyond Colly's line of sight. What were they doing?

A low rumble made Colly's blood freeze. The *chug-chug* of an engine followed by the clanking of chains started his heart pounding. He peered at the spot where Jaz had disappeared on the barge. "Hurry!" he shouted inside his head. Where was she? Why didn't she get off?

Maybe she was trying.

Maybe she was caught!

He took out his red whistle and gave a short careful toot. No Jaz.

He tooted again, louder and longer this time.

Nothing.

As the tug pulled away, Colly saw a face staring back at him through a small window in the cabin under the wheelhouse.

It was Harvey Chiapot!

Chapter Eight

He knew it! The guy was just too nasty a piece of work not be involved in something illegal.

Colly's blood snap-crackled through his veins as he watched the barge pull away. Where was Jaz? Maybe she had hopped off the other side and was waiting next to the dock. Yes, that had to be it. As soon as it was safe, she would pop her head up over the side and wave to him.

But why was the tug leaving now? It wasn't scheduled to go for at least another hour!

Then again…there was the fake emergency. What better time to get away with something in plain sight than when the whole town was busy with something else? No one had known in advance when the fake emergency would be, but maybe Harvey had decided to take advantage of it and get out while the getting was good.

The tug chugged into the harbor, the barge swinging out behind it. Colly stared at the edge of the dock, willing Jaz to appear. As soon as the tug was on course, he dashed to where he hoped Jaz would be waiting. "Jaz!" he shouted. He peered over the edge.

Nothing. She wasn't there. She was trapped on the barge, heading to wherever Harvey was hiding the birds, and then possibly to a waiting ship.

With an icy sickness in his belly, Colly realized that he had no idea where that would be. There had been no coordinates on the clipboard. He glanced around, hoping to see his uncle or someone else who might help, but the dock was empty.

There was no time to hesitate and no time to think things through. He had to follow! Sprinting from the dock, he began running along the shore after the tug and barge, stumbling over rocks. Tooting the whistle again and again, hoping someone would hear, he didn't dare stop his chase. He would keep the tug in sight if it killed him!

He needed Uncle Norbert and the JCRs! He needed the RCMP! "Stop!" he bellowed. He tooted the whistle again. "Someone stop that tug!"

Running hard, grunting as he turned his ankles one way and then another on the stones, he could hear his heart pounding in his ears. He gasped for breath as the tug drew farther and farther away. Even as it disappeared from his sight, he kept running.

He felt a hard lump building in the back of his throat. Why had he let Jaz check out the barge? She was like a trouble magnet. He should have guessed something would go wrong!

It should have been him on that barge. He should be the one in danger.

He swallowed.

Maybe it was because of his blue eyes, except this time the curse had bounced over to Jaz.

"Stop it, Colly!" he muttered. Nothing bad was going to happen. He wouldn't let it.

A stitch in his side had zapped all the wind he had left. He stopped and looked around. He was beyond sight of the town, and there was no sign of the tug. He couldn't even hear it.

He did hear something else, though. A motorboat! He stared in the direction the sound was coming from. A moment later he spotted it.

"Over here!" he shouted, jumping up and down and waving his hands in the air. "Help! Come over here!"

As the boat drew closer, slapping the white-caps in its path, he could see a lone figure wearing a green sweatshirt with a red logo—a JCR sweatshirt! Underneath the matching green ball cap he could see a face split in two with a grin. It was Tommy!

"Hey man, what are you doing out here?" Tommy asked as he drew close and cut the engine. "Grandfather said he saw you taking off this way, blowing a whistle. He gave me his boat so I could catch you!"

"It's Jaz!" Colly called, splashing out to meet him. The water was icy, but he didn't care. "We've got to follow the tug that just left. She's on the barge!"

"What tug?"

"It left the harbor at the same time your grandfather saw me running," Colly said. "But I don't know where it's headed. We've got to find it and then go for help."

He climbed in and looked around the bottom of the boat. There was a life jacket, but it looked like it was meant for a three-year-old. "Have you got another life jacket?"

"No, sorry," Tommy said. "That one is for my little cousin. You want mine?"

"No…it's okay," Colly said, trying to shrug it off like it was no big deal. "We'll probably be staying close to shore."

As quickly as he could, he explained what they'd read on the clipboard in the Radio Dispatch office, and how they became suspicious of this particular tug and Harvey Chiapot.

"And you think Harvey is the poacher?" Tommy asked, his smile now gone, as he gunned the boat back into gear.

Colly nodded. "At first it was just a guess, but when I saw him in the window of the tug I knew for sure."

Tommy frowned, his brows knitting together awkwardly, as if it were something they were not used to doing. This was the first time Colly had seen Tommy without a smile on his face.

"Harvey took over the hotel two years ago. He's a little strange sometimes, but he doesn't seem like a criminal."

"Lots of criminals don't seem like criminals. Think about it. Maybe he just moved here to work out his plan!"

"I don't know..." Tommy looked troubled. "Maybe—maybe not."

"You have to admit it's strange. The feather, and then the tug with no destination. Why would Chiapot be on that tug if he wasn't up to something?"

"I don't know," Tommy said. It didn't look like he wanted to talk anymore. Colly didn't feel like talking either. His chest was so tight with worry he could hardly breathe. He scanned the open sea for signs of the tug. There were clouds blowing in again, looking like little knots of steel wool against a sea of blue. What if the weather turned bad and it started raining? It would be even harder to find them then.

They passed the place where they'd picnicked earlier in the day. It felt like so long ago.

"Let's go to the pingo!" Colly cried. "We'll be able to see more from there!"

"Good idea," Tommy said, turning the boat toward the beach.

As fast as they could, they pulled the boat safely up on the beach and sprinted up the side of the pingo.

Chest heaving as he ran, Colly looked out to sea as often as he could without losing his step. He did slip and land on his chin a few times, but it didn't matter. He kept climbing.

Halfway up, he saw something. "Look!" he cried, grabbing Tommy's arm.

In the distance, they could easily make out the dark smudge of an ocean liner. "We were right!" Colly said. "It's got to be meeting the *Stampe Collector*. Why else would it be sitting there?"

"I don't see the tug," Tommy said, squinting and shielding his eyes with one hand.

"I wish we had my uncle's field glasses," Colly said.

"I wish we had a radio!" Tommy looked like he was angry with himself. "When Grandfather told me to take his boat, I didn't stop to think."

"You didn't know what was wrong. I just wish we knew where the tug went!"

"It must have gone into a bay somewhere," Tommy said. "Maybe we can't see it because it's behind a pingo or a hill."

"They have to come out eventually," Colly muttered.

"Wherever they are, hopefully Jaz has enough sense to get off the barge before she ends up stuck at sea!"

Yeah, Jaz and sense, Colly thought. Not so much. Out loud he said, "She'll probably only get off if she thinks we'll find her."

Suddenly, from directly behind them, there was a tooth-rattling, nails-against-blackboard squawk.

Chapter Nine

"Man, I HATE that bird!" Tommy cried as they watched the blue-eyed raven waddle toward them.

"Maybe he's out here looking for his owner," Colly said.

Tommy's whole face lit up. "Let's bring him back to the boat. If that raven feather with the dead gyrfalcons really was from Beastie, then maybe he knows where Harvey is going!"

Just as he'd seen Harvey do, Colly offered Beastie his arm. "Good bird," he said, when Beastie hopped onto it. He stepped carefully as they made their way back down the pingo, hoping the bird wouldn't fly away. Just as the pinch of his talons was becoming unbearable, Beastie shifted his weight and extended his beak toward Colly's mouth.

Tommy snorted. "I think he wants you to kiss him!"

Colly turned his head away. "No way!"

"You better do it," Tommy said. "We don't want him to get mad and fly home!"

Colly looked at Beastie, who was opening and closing his beak, still leaning toward him. "Oh, fine!" He lifted his chin and gave Beastie a loud smack on the beak. "Nice Beastie," he said; then he spat and wiped his mouth with his sleeve.

Beastie gave a soft squawk and a few musical *pinging* sounds, as if he were pleased. He must not have liked the sound of the boat, though. As soon as Tommy increased the power, the bird flew in the air.

"Find Harvey!" Colly shouted.

The bird appeared to understand, or maybe he was just continuing along a path he'd been on all along. He flew along the shore as Tommy and Colly followed in the boat as best they could. There were so many small bays and inlets, they had to strain to see him as they sped along. In places the shore had what looked like ice-filled cliffs, dark on top and white underneath, as if a piece had broken away, exposing the permafrost. Kind of like a giant gobstopper candy that had been smacked with a hammer.

They watched as Beastie flew higher, and then turned and flew inland. A moment later they saw him swoop from the sky and land somewhere out of sight.

"Oh great," Tommy said.

Colly scanned the shore. Ice-filled cliffs and grassy hillocks made it difficult to see very far inland. A little farther on, the shore offered a few more boggy inlets—a chance to take the boat a little closer to where the bird must have landed. "Let's try in there," he said, pointing.

Slowly, Tommy chugged into the opening, where they found nothing but bog and brush.

"Try the next one," Colly said, his voice tight. "Beastie must have seen something to make him stop!"

As the boat sped around the weedy curve, Colly spotted something on the muddy shore. Philip's windsurfer!

"Why would Philip be out here?" Colly asked.

"He goes all over for his wind research," Tommy said. "If Philip is out here, maybe he has a radio or a satellite phone and can call for help!"

Colly nodded. "That's a good idea."

As soon as they were close enough to the shore, they jumped into the frigid water and secured the boat. Beyond the beach, Colly climbed a small ridge made of mud and permafrost. "Philip!" he called. He listened. Nothing. He climbed back down.

Tommy shrugged. "He's got to be here somewhere."

Colly put his hand up, testing the wind. "It's shifted. Before it was coming from the northwest, and now it's from the southeast," he said. "Unless it shifts again, it's only going to carry our voices out to sea. If Philip is a little bit inland, he won't hear us."

"He wouldn't have gone far on foot," Tommy said, looking around. He pointed east. "I'll go look around that hill over there, okay?"

"Sure. I'll stick to the shore and head west. If you see him, shout. The wind will be behind you, and I'll hear you. If I find him first, we'll meet you on the hill."

There was no time to waste. They each took off at a stumbling trot over bog, moss and stone—Tommy over a crest, and Colly continuing west along the shore.

"Philip!" Colly called. His feet were wet and freezing. Mud sucked at them with every step. A ridge of earth and ice beside him made it impossible to see where Tommy had gone. Because of the curve to the shoreline, he couldn't even see where they'd landed the boat. "Philip!" he called again, louder.

Nothing. The harder he listened the more he could only hear the wind whipping his jacket and beating the insides of his ear canals like some extra-enthusiastic drum band in a parade.

It sure didn't seem like there was anyone else around. He climbed up the ridge of mud and permafrost and looked. There was the hill where Tommy had gone. But where was Tommy? He took a deep breath. Maybe he'd climbed down the other side.

A knot was building in his stomach. Why were they wasting time looking for Philip? It was possible that he wasn't even here. Maybe the wind had pushed his board out to sea and then up the coast.

They should have gone back for help while they were still close to town. Like his father always said, hindsight was a kick in the pants.

"Tommy!" he called, knowing the wind was whipping his voice in the wrong direction.

He needed to get to the hill. Cutting across the tundra, he bounded from one spongy bit of bog to the next. Finally he reached the hill and clambered up the side of it. No Tommy. No Philip. He looked in all directions. Tundra, tundra, hills and sea, but no sign of anyone, anywhere.

Where was Tommy?

"Tommy!" he shouted, trying to keep a panicky squeak from his voice.

Wind blew in and around his ears, deafening him. He turned his head and covered the ear facing into the wind, hoping it would help him hear.

His stomach flipped. "Tommy!" he bellowed as loud as he could. "Tommy!"

He looked back toward where they had pulled the boat to shore. No boat. It was gone. So was Tommy.

He swallowed, hard.

Had Tommy run into trouble? Had he taken the boat and gone looking for him? He scanned the shore in the direction Tommy had disappeared. Nothing. Even from this vantage point, there were rocks and hills that might be hiding the little boat. Still, Tommy should be able to hear his voice.

Unless the sound of the boat's engine was blocking it out.

Yes…that must be it.

Colly took a deep breath, reached into his pocket and clutched his red JCR whistle. Tommy might not be able to hear his voice, but surely he would hear the whistle. Colly blew into it as hard as he could and with all the frustration he was feeling. Then he crumpled to the rock, teeth chattering. He took quick shallow breaths. With a start, he realized he was on the edge of panic. That was no good. Panicking wouldn't help him, and it wouldn't help Jaz. He took in as deep a breath as his lungs could handle and let it out, slowly. Then he did it again. And again.

He scrambled back down the hill and began running as fast as he could toward the shore. Tommy must have gone looking for him. Maybe he'd found Philip, and they were both looking for him.

Back at the muddy beach, he looked around. He blinked, not trusting what he saw—or rather, didn't see.

Philip's windsurfing board was gone. He tried to remember whether it had been there when he had noticed the boat was gone.

It didn't matter. Tommy and Philip must have gone for help! They were probably looking to pick him up along the shoreline.

A squawk directly behind him brought his panic to the surface again, but only for a moment. "Hello, Beastie," he said, greeting the raven as it landed a few feet from him and waddled toward him. "I guess it's just you and me."

"And me," a voice said.

It was Harvey Chiapot.

Chapter Ten

Colly opened his mouth to speak, but nothing came out. It was like he was seeing things, because what he was seeing didn't make sense. Harvey wasn't supposed to be here…he was supposed to be on the tug, smuggling his birds!

"So he dumped you here too, hey?" Harvey asked. He pulled a small plastic container of green mints from his pocket, gave them a shake and offered one to Colly.

Colly shook his head to the mints and found his voice. "What are you talking about?" he asked, scrambling to grab hold of his wits. He backed up and reached for a piece of driftwood. It wasn't much of a weapon, but it was the only thing within reach. He raised it above his head.

Harvey looked at the stick and laughed. He popped a few mints into his mouth and crunched them. "Are you gonna hit me with that, kid? Why?" He shook his head. "I've been through much worse, believe me."

"Where's Jaz?" Colly asked, his voice harsh.

"Jaz? You mean that little girl you were with? How should I know?"

"You were on the tug. You're a poacher!"

"Look, kid, I don't know anything about poachers, but it was Philip who dumped me on the boat. Him, or one of those thugs he was with."

"Philip?"

"All I know is that I was bringing a bowl of chili to Philip in his room, just because I thought he might like it. It's my mom's recipe, you know. From back home…"

"And he locked you on the tug for that?"

"The chili? No! He didn't even taste it. At least I don't think so. Like I said, I brought him up a bowl and saw his door was open, so I walked right in. He was there with two big fellas. They had a map spread out on the table…and something else." He paused and rubbed his chin.

Colly's arm was beginning to ache from holding the driftwood above his head, but he kept it steady. It was a detailed story, but it was possible Harvey was making it up on the spot. "What did you see?"

Harvey frowned. "I'm thinking, kid. It's kind of fuzzy, probably because one of those guys hit me. Left hook, I think, and a pretty good one."

"Why would he do that?"

Harvey snapped his fingers. "I remember. It was because the other big guy was holding a dead gyrfalcon! His hand was all wrapped in bandages. He was telling Philip that the birds were vicious, and that he wasn't going to feed them anymore."

Colly lowered the driftwood a little, stunned. "That can't be true."

"He said they were going to get them loaded right now, and that Philip could catch up with them on his windsurfer. Then they saw me, and I got hit before I could even say anything. Knocked me out. Next thing I know, I'm on that tug."

Colly's head was spinning. He set his feet apart to better steady himself. He felt like he was climbing up a rope ladder, and someone had just shaken it.

"Look, kid, whatever's going on, it has nothing to do with me. It's Philip you should be talking to." Harvey stopped and scanned the shore. "He was here a minute ago. Didn't you see him?"

"Philip was the one who dumped you here?"

"Not exactly. It was his goons—the big guys with him in his room. Philip wasn't on the tug, but he *was* here. He showed up ten or fifteen minutes after the goons left me here blindfolded and tied up tighter than my beef-wrapped asparagus."

"Tighter than…what?"

"My own special recipe, kid. I serve it in the café." He shook a few more mints into his mouth and crunched them. This time Colly noticed Harvey's wrists. They were red and raw.

"Philip could've helped me, but he didn't." He shook his head. "I thought we were friends. He wouldn't even take off my blindfold and look me in the eye."

Colly didn't want to believe it. "What did he say?"

"Not much, actually. He thanked me for making him a rich man."

"You made Philip rich? How?"

"Dunno."

It was hard to accept. Philip was such a nice man… and Harvey was not. "You've known him a long time, right?"

"We never kept in touch. Actually, when we were kids in California, he was pretty mean to me, even though I was two years older than him. It was like he was always trying to show people how tough he was." Harvey took a deep breath, and let it out slowly. "I thought he'd changed."

"How can I be sure you're not lying?" Colly asked.

"I'm not. Whatever this is about, Philip is in the thick of it. Otherwise he would've helped me, right?"

"But you're the one who's crazy about birds. If anyone is smuggling gyrfalcons, it makes sense that it's you."

"So that's what this is about? Philip likes gyrfalcons too. That's how I ran into him. We were both at a Birds of Prey convention."

Slowly, Colly nodded. "In Denver."

Harvey raised his eyebrows. "How did you know?"

"Philip told us."

"At least he told the truth about something," Harvey muttered.

Colly saw Harvey was soaked to the shins, as if he'd stumbled and fallen into the water.

"How did you get free?" Colly asked.

Harvey shrugged. "At first my head hurt too much to even try, but Beastie here found me and helped by picking at the blindfold." He turned to the bird and stroked the back of its head. "He's pretty smart, you know. Anyway, after I could see, I just rubbed my wrists against a rock. After a corner of the tape came free, it was pretty easy."

Colly looked closer and saw blood. "Do they hurt?"

"Yeah, but at least I'm free. Tied up like that I could have been toast…maybe even a whole meal for a wandering bear."

"I ran right past here and didn't see you. Where were you?"

Harvey gestured. "Not far—about fifty feet that way. I was sure glad to hear you blow that whistle!"

Colly swallowed. It must be true. He'd always relied on his gut to help him sort things out, and his gut said Harvey was telling the truth. Harvey was the good guy in this—or at least, a victim.

Harvey sighed. "Look, kid, I guess I don't much care whether or not you believe me. I figure I've got about a two-hour hike back to town, so I'm going to get going. Come if you want to. If you don't…well, unless you got some other way back, I think you're crazy."

Colly lowered the stick of driftwood. "I believe you," he said, "but I can't go back. Not yet."

"Why not?"

"I've got to find out where that tug went. Jaz's life might depend on it." He paused. "Maybe Tommy's too."

"Tommy?" Harvey looked hard at Colly, then out to sea, and then back at Colly again. "What have you kids been up to?"

As quickly as he could, Colly explained how Jaz had gotten stuck on the barge, and how he and Tommy had tried to give chase. "We split up to look for Philip after we found his windsurfing board," Colly said, frowning. "I guess Tommy found him."

Harvey rubbed the back of his neck. "I suppose it's possible. Maybe Philip took him somewhere to finish him off."

Colly felt like throwing up. "No…if he wanted to do that he would have just done it here, right?"

Harvey looked at him, softening, as if realizing that his words might have been upsetting to Colly. "You're probably right, kid." He patted him on the shoulder, but to Colly it felt awkward, as if Harvey wasn't used to offering comfort.

Colly scanned the water once again, feeling hope sink beneath the waves lapping against the empty shore.

Chapter Eleven

Harvey shrugged. "Not much we can do except head back to town," he said. "We'll get some help there."

Colly tried to swallow the lump in his throat. "That'll take too long. Tommy and Jaz are in danger!"

"We don't know where they went, kid."

Colly looked at Beastie, who looked back at him, cocking his head to the side, as if listening. "Before this happened, Tommy and I were hoping Beastie would show us where the tug went."

"Why would he do that?"

"Because you were on the tug. We figured that wherever the tug was going, you'd probably been there before."

Harvey frowned. "Because you thought I was a poacher?"

"Yeah."

Harvey sighed. "I can't head back to town and leave you running off to who knows where. You want me to send Beastie after Philip right now?"

"You can do that?"

"Maybe," Harvey said. "It started out as a game we played, and I turned it into training. I thought maybe Philip and I could send messages to each other, sort of in place of cell phone service." He frowned. "But that was when I thought we were friends."

"Send Beastie after him, please," Colly pleaded. "We've got to catch the tug before it heads out to sea. It's our best chance!"

"What then?"

"We'll sneak Jaz off while they're busy with the gyrfalcons and then figure out what they did with Tommy."

Harvey frowned and then nodded. "Worth a try," he said. He lifted his arm for Beastie, whispered in the bird's ear and flung him into the air. They watched as the bird rose high above them, circled a few times, and then took off slightly inland. "Looks like Beastie found a shortcut," Harvey said. "Come on!"

They began slogging over the tundra—moss, grass, flowers and puddles. Colly stumbled as he tried to keep his eye on the bird, but kept moving forward. Even though the sky had clouded over, it was bright, and his eyes were soon watering. It must be high cloud. Good. That meant it wouldn't rain. The last thing they needed was more wetness. He was already soaked through.

He tried to run faster as the bird flew farther and farther away. Finally he was forced to admit he was staring only at the memory of it. Chest heaving, he tripped over a hillock and crumpled to the ground.

"You okay?" he heard from somewhere behind him. Harvey was puffing as he caught up. "Don't worry, we'll get there."

Colly felt a hard lump in his throat. He'd never felt closer to sobbing than he did now. "No, we won't," he said. "Beastie is gone."

"Not really. He'll be back if he doesn't see us. And in the meantime, we've got a pingo to aim for," Harvey said, pointing.

Colly looked. Sure enough, not too far away there was a pingo.

Harvey offered him a hand. "Come on."

"Wait," Colly said, pulling the map out of his back pocket. He traced the coastline, finding first the pingo where they'd picnicked earlier that day, then the place where Harvey had found him, and finally the pingo where they were headed. "This could be it!" he said in a rush. "See how a channel leads from the Beaufort Sea to this bay? This must be where the tug is!"

"Could be," Harvey said as they began jogging again—a little more slowly than before, but steadily. "I just can't get my head around all this," he muttered. "I know Philip left me on the tundra, but it's hard to believe he's a poacher."

"It's possible that he planned this when he was at the Birds of Prey convention," Colly said. "Did he talk about gyrfalcons?"

Harvey nodded. "A bit. In a session talking about habitat, I told him I'd found a nesting place for white-phase gyrfalcons."

"Are white-phase gyrfalcons special?"

"They're unusual for this part of the coast." Harvey slapped his head and began muttering.

"What is it?"

"Well…he told me white gyrfalcons were worth a lot of money to some people. At the time I didn't think much about it. I guess I was just so glad he grew up to be such a nice friendly fellow."

"He fooled everyone."

"Yeah, but it's my fault he's here. He was pretty interested in Tuk, so I told him everything I could think of. I told him the town was interested in setting up a wind farm, and he told me he was a wind researcher. It all seemed so perfect. I was the one who put him in touch with the town council."

As Harvey talked, Colly thought about something his dad always said. *If something seems too good to be true, it probably is.* He didn't say it out loud though. It was obvious Harvey felt bad enough.

"I thought Philip loved birds, same as me," Harvey said. "Thought that's why he was at the convention. Not to find a way to make money off of 'em."

Seeing Harvey's obvious distress at the thought that the gyrfalcons might have been deliberately captured and harmed, Colly felt sorry for him. "Sometimes you just can't tell about people," he said, feeling the truth of the words snug up around him like a blanket.

They were almost at the pingo. It wasn't as large as the ones he'd seen closer to Tuk, but it gave them something to aim for. If it was big enough to hide a tug, it was big enough for them to hide behind once they got there. Colly tapped the map and pointed. "We should come at it from the south side."

They picked a path around the pingo until they found a spot they could watch from without being seen. At least, that was the plan. It was a shallow, grass-and dirt-covered rift—not the best hiding place, but it would do. As long as they stayed still and quiet, they should be safe.

Colly's blue eyes grew wide as he peeked around the edge of it. "There it is!" he breathed.

Chapter Twelve

Relief mixed with anxiety made soup of Colly's guts as he stared at the tug and barge. Two men made their way down a ramp off the barge onto a muddy beach and headed toward the pingo. To Colly, it looked like someone had taken a bite out of the pingo, creating an opening to an icy cave. He wondered if this was the one Tommy's grandfather had told them about—the one he had used as a meat freezer.

A man walked out of the cave. Philip was easy to recognize with his blond hair and black wet suit with yellow stripes. He looked like a hornet.

And there was Beastie. He was hopping on the path close by. Philip stopped. It looked like he was talking to him.

But where were Tommy and Jaz?

"We've got to stop him!" Colly whispered. The wind was coming from the southwest, and there was a risk it would carry his voice to Philip or someone on the tug. That would be a very bad thing.

Harvey nodded. "I know. But let's think before we do anything rash." He poked his head back up over the edge.

"Careful," Colly murmured, and Harvey pulled back a little.

There was a sudden flutter of black close to the pingo opening. It was Beastie! It looked like he was looking their way.

Alarm flared in Colly's belly as the bird squawked, and then flew high in the air and circled toward them.

Unfortunately, Philip was watching Beastie too.

"He's going to give us away!" Colly hissed.

Harvey shoved him back. "Stay hidden, kid."

Before Colly could stop him, Harvey launched himself from their hiding place and trotted down the side of the pingo toward Philip. He stopped about twenty feet away as Philip and two burly men in coveralls—one of them with his hand wrapped in white bandages—rushed up the side of the pingo toward him.

He must have wanted to be close enough for Colly to hear. When the men grabbed him, he didn't struggle.

Colly flattened himself in the grass, and pushed aside a tangle of purple wildflowers and silver-leafed Labrador tea to see.

"You shouldn't have come here," Philip snarled. "Why didn't you just go back to town?"

"I need to understand why you did this," Harvey said.

Slowly, Philip smiled. "But, Harvey, this was all your idea."

"What…you dumping me on the tundra?"

Philip sighed noisily as he shook his head. "It was fate, running into you at that convention."

"I thought so too. We both like birds."

"Yes, but our goals are very different. Did you know that gyrfalcons are prized as sport birds?"

"Well, sure—at least, they used to be. Falconry was pretty popular during the Middle Ages."

"It still is, in some circles. Some very *rich* circles. And some of these very rich circles are willing to pay big money for gyrfalcons."

"It's not worth it, Philip. You ought to know that. You'll go to jail!"

"Only if I get caught. I've got a king in Saudi Arabia willing to pay me ten thousand dollars per bird. Even more if I deliver him a white female."

Harvey was shaking his head. "But gyrfalcons aren't easy to capture, and when they *are* captured, they don't often survive."

"Catch enough of them, and it doesn't matter. Who cares about a few dead birds?"

Colly's blood boiled at Philip's words. Harvey's must have been boiling too. He was straining against his captors as if he'd like to jump on Philip and teach him a lesson.

"What about the dead musk ox? Was that you too?"

Philip nodded. "When people started finding the birds, I figured I needed a diversion."

There it was. The musk ox was a decoy, something to distract people while gyrfalcons were being caught and sold illegally. It was just as Colly guessed, but with a different bad guy.

"I'll give you one chance, *old friend*." Philip's voice was dripping sarcasm.

"What?"

"You know more about birds and keeping them alive than I do. Come with me, and I'll cut you in."

Harvey was shaking his head even before Philip finished speaking. "You can't do this, Philip. What you're doing is wrong!"

"I'll take that as a 'no.' Suit yourself."

"They'll figure it out, you know."

Philip shrugged. "Not before I'm far, far away. While Beastie and the rest of his raven buddies are picking the rotting meat from your bones, I'll be hanging out with Saudi royalty."

Colly shivered, waiting for Harvey to react. But he said nothing. He didn't move at all. Had he given up?

Philip seemed annoyed at Harvey's lack of response. "Enough of this," he said, his voice suddenly harsh. "Put him with the boy."

Alarm shot through Colly's body as he flattened himself, fearful that he'd been discovered. Then he realized…Philip was talking about Tommy! He forgot to breathe as the other men dragged Harvey toward the opening into the pingo.

So, Tommy was inside the pingo. But where was Jaz? She might be in the pingo with Tommy, or…he stared hard at the barge. Could she still be hidden on board? If she was, then she was still okay.

As if she knew he was waiting, she suddenly appeared between two stacked boxes. How had she fit in such a tiny space? It looked like she might be planning on making a run for it. Unfortunately, one of the crewmen who'd helped drag Harvey inside the pingo reappeared, jogged up the ramp and walked along the side of the barge toward her. She ducked back out of sight.

Good, he thought. Wait for your chance, Jaz. Keep watching, and then jump!

He watched as Philip and three other men loaded four large crates into the shed-sized container. The birds! They were screaming, obviously upset. After placing the cages into the larger crate, Philip slammed the door shut, but didn't bother with the lock. Colly guessed that was because from here, he was heading straight out to sea and the waiting ship.

Jaz had to get off the barge! Now!

As the tug started chugging, pulling the barge away from the pingo, he hoped to see Jaz tumbling over the edge of it and swimming for shore. But he didn't. He thought about taking a chance and running after the barge, but something stopped him dead.

Smoke. It was coming from inside the pingo!

There wasn't a lot of it, but even a small fire couldn't be good inside a pingo. If the ice inside melted, the outside would collapse…trapping Tommy and Harvey inside!

Chapter Thirteen

He wanted to pull his hair out as the tug moved slowly away.

Jaz…or the pingo?

Jaz…or the pingo?

If only he could run both ways at once!

As much as he feared for Jaz, a fire inside the pingo was even more urgent.

He had to help Tommy and Harvey. Now.

Sick at not going after Jaz first, he dashed toward the pingo. He kept low to the ground, hoping to blend in with the flowers and willow shrubs, until finally, he was at the entrance. He touched the side of it. Tiny crystals like bunched-up diamonds framed the opening. They fell away at his touch. The pingo was already damaged. "Tommy!" he shouted. "Harvey!"

"We're locked up in here, kid!" Harvey shouted back. "Come and get us while you can!"

The light from the fire should have made it easier to see, but the smoke made his eyes burn. He rubbed them and spotted what looked like a cage, with two people pressed up against the door.

"Put out the fire!" Tommy cried.

"Right!" He looked around for something to scoop water with. He spotted a flash of color and raced toward it—Philip's windsurfing board! He unhitched the fabric sail and rushed outside to the water, where he scooped up as much as he could. It was no good. The water all sloshed out before he even made it to the opening of the pingo! He turned to try again, but stopped. The ice crystals! Solid was much easier to carry than liquid. He scraped and scooped as much as he could from the opening, then rushed to the fire and dumped it on. The fire sizzled as the crystals turned from solid to liquid, and then to steamy gas. The wood, now wet, smoked even more. He bent double, coughing, and kicked at the logs until they scattered. They were still glowing in places, but at least the flames were out. There was still plenty of light coming in from the cave opening. He sprinted toward the cage holding Tommy and Harvey. There were several large cages, all made of wooden posts and two-by-two boards, but the one they were in was right at the back and in the middle.

"Hurry up, kid," Harvey said. His voice sounded tight.

Colly rattled the lock on the door. "What do I do?" he asked, looking about. "We need something to break the lock!"

"You'd better find something quick," Tommy said. "You hear that dripping?"

Colly listened. Yes. It was there, a steady *drip-drip-drip*. The fire was out, but it had damaged the pingo. That, and probably the extra digging Philip had done in hollowing out the old meat freezer to make room for falcon cages, had left the space unstable. He had to get Tommy and Harvey out quickly, before the pingo collapsed.

He spotted the windsurfer. It wasn't heavy or firm enough to smash a lock, but maybe he could use it another way. "Check all the bars. Look for a loose one!"

Between the three of them they shook each and every bar on all four sides.

"No good, kid, they're all pretty firm."

"Check the top!"

Since Harvey was the only one tall enough to get a good grasp on the top bars, Colly and Tommy waited as he shook one after another, all the while listening to the *drip-drip-drip* of water all around.

"This one!" Harvey cried. He put all his weight on it and began swinging. He was right—it was loose. Colly grasped the windsurfer and ran back to the cage. "Give me a leg up," he said. "I'll try and use this as a lever and see if I can flip the bar out from the top."

Tommy and Harvey made one cup with their four hands. Colly stepped in it and felt himself being lifted to the top. He was lifted with so much energy, it was like he was being launched, and he had to grab at the top to keep from being flung too far. As soon as he was balanced, he stuck the board between the bars. Now he needed something to slip underneath the board to give it something to rock against as he levered up the bar. "Harvey—give me your boots!" Harvey must have realized what he needed, because he didn't argue.

A moment later the boots were underneath the middle of the board.

"Hurry!" Tommy cried.

"I am," he said through gritted teeth. "Don't worry."

He leaned all his weight against the free side and hoped. There was a creak, then a snap and finally the bar came free!

It wasn't a wide gap, but it was enough to get through.

"You go first," Tommy said, offering Harvey a leg up. A minute later, with a grunt, Tommy was up as well.

Colly handed Harvey back his boots. "Don't forget these," he said.

"Let's get out of here," Harvey said. With dripping sounds all around, they raced to the opening. As they burst into the open air, they were met with a squawk. Beastie!

"I've never been so glad to see that bird," Tommy said.

"Wait a minute!" Harvey said, dashing back inside.

"What are you doing?" Colly shouted. "It's not safe!"

A moment later, Harvey reappeared. He was carrying Philip's windsurfer—with the sail. "I thought we might need this. If one of you boys knows how to use it, you can get help a lot quicker than we can by walking."

"Wait," Colly said, looking up and down the beach. "Tommy, where's your boat?"

"Philip got the crew from the tug to bash a hole in it. They sank it in the middle of this bay."

"What about the life jackets?"

Tommy shrugged. "Must have taken them with him."

"So?" Harvey said. "Who's going for help? Want to draw straws?" He glanced about. "Guess we're out of luck on the straws."

Tommy looked at Colly. "You caught on pretty quick when Philip gave us that lesson," he said. "You should go."

Colly felt all the blood drain from his face. He began shivering, though it wasn't from any chill in the air.

"What's wrong?" Tommy asked.

"I…" Colly began. He swallowed. "Nothing. Give me the board." Harvey handed it to him. His hands felt slippery as he gripped it. He wiped them against his shirt and grabbed hold again. His heart was beating so loudly it muted the sounds of wind and sea. He dropped the board. "I can't," he said.

"Why not?" Harvey asked.

"I…I don't have a life jacket," he mumbled.

"But it's our best shot," Tommy said. "Are you scared?"

His first reaction was to deny it. After all, they didn't know about the curse. Instead he cleared his throat. "My cousin drowned last month. He wasn't wearing a life jacket."

"Oh Jeez, man. I'm really sorry to hear that. Okay, no problem," Tommy said, grabbing hold of the board. "I'll do it."

But as Tommy splashed into the water and tried balancing on the board, it was clear that it would take him time to get the hang of it. Too much time.

Colly took a deep breath. Sometimes you just had to make yourself do things, even if you were afraid. "Let me try," he said. He took the board from Tommy. After a few fumbles, it felt like he might be able to do it. A few tries after that, and he had it.

"I guess it's me," he said.

Chapter Fourteen

"Are you still scared?" Tommy asked.

"It doesn't matter. I have to do this," Colly said. But his body wasn't listening. His knees turned to jelly, and he sat. He leaned forward, putting his head in his hands, trying to steady his breathing.

It was more than not having a life jacket, and it was more than just being scared. It was the curse! Just as it had happened to Junie and the other blue-eyed boys who came before him, it could happen to Colly. It could happen to Colly *now*.

But what about Jaz? He couldn't jam out now! He had to help her! But it was like he wasn't in control of his body. It was controlling him.

Harvey patted him on the back. "Well, of course you're scared, kid. If Philip was willing to bury me and Tommy alive, you can bet he won't think twice about tossing Jaz to the whales!"

"You're not helping!" Colly shouted.

Tommy and Harvey sat in silence on either side of Colly. Waiting.

"I've been in scary situations before," Colly said.

"You mean like during the JCR dog derby?" Tommy asked.

"But that turned out great. Some people even called us heroes."

"The thing about being scared," Harvey said, "is that sometimes it creeps up on you. I don't know what happened during this dog derby you're talking about, but I'm guessing things happened pretty fast. Maybe too fast to be scared. Am I right?"

Colly nodded.

"Think of it this way, kid. Things are happening pretty fast now too, but this time your body is ready. It might feel like your body is controlling you, instead of the other way around, but really it only wants to make good and sure you know how scared you are. Fear is the body's way of staying safe."

"So what do I do? I still have to get this done."

Harvey shrugged. "Never mind what *might* happen, you can only deal with what *is* happening right here, right now. Respect your fear, and it will serve you."

Colly thought about it. Finally, gripping the board, he stood. He took a deep breath in and blew it out. "Right here, right now," he said. "Jaz needs me. It's time to get this done."

"You can follow the shore all to way to town," Harvey said. "Stay close to land, and you'll be fine. We'll head out on foot and get there after you, but at least you can get help for your friend.

He shook his head. "I'm not going to town. I've got to catch the barge."

"You can't!" Tommy shouted. "It's too dangerous. And like you said, you don't have a life jacket."

Colly looked at the sky. "If only there were people looking for us instead of pretend boaters, we could signal a search plane."

Tommy snapped his fingers and looked at his watch. "That's it!" he said. He put his hand in the air, testing the wind. "Remember what your uncle was telling us this morning?"

"Yeah…it was about ground-to-air signals."

"He also told us that airplanes land *into* the wind. I know from all the times I've seen it that the regular flight sometimes swings over this way. I never understood why, but now I know it must do that when the wind is coming from the southeast. Like right now."

Excitement sparked overtop Colly's fear. "What time does the plane come in?"

"Pretty soon," Tommy said. "We'll try and get its attention, and you go and catch that barge!"

"Right!"

"I don't understand," Harvey said.

Tommy turned to him. "In JCRs, we learned how to make a distress signal that a pilot can see from the air. If we move fast, we can do that before the plane comes by."

"And if I can get to Jaz before they get out to the ship," Colly said, "I'm pretty sure we can fit the two of us on this board."

"Are you sure? Tommy said, doubtfully. "I think it's built for one. What about balance?"

"Jaz is small," Colly said. "Besides, we don't have a choice. If we can't sail, we'll just hang onto the board and float until someone picks us up."

"Let's hope it doesn't come to that," Harvey said. "That water is pretty cold."

"Come on!" Tommy cried, running along the shore, picking up large white stones. "Let's do this." He stopped and looked back at Colly. "Are you sure you're okay?"

Colly took a deep breath, surprised that his heart wasn't pounding quite as hard as before. He was still scared, but he felt he could do this. He would stay watchful and upright. His fear of falling, and worse, his fear of failing, would help him get this done. It had to.

"I'm good," Colly said, giving Tommy a thumbs-up.

As Harvey and Tommy scrambled over rocky shore and soggy moss picking up suitable rocks, Colly thought hard about what Philip had taught him. Taking one more deep, steadying breath, he pushed the board into the water and climbed on. He leaned one way and then another, trying to catch his balance as the wind caught the sail. After a moment he straightened the board and was away!

"Good luck, kid!" he heard Harvey call, and then his voice was lost to the wind that beat about his head, finding its way into his ears and making them ache.

He turned his head slightly, hoping for relief, and nearly capsized the board. He gritted his teeth, faced forward and accepted the pain.

Before long, his muscles were screaming, and his fingers felt frozen in place. With a start he realized that he'd been concentrating so hard on what he was doing, he hadn't had time to worry about the curse. He was too busy just trying to hang on!

He heard a rumble that made his back teeth buzz. Glancing up, he saw it was an airplane! He had no idea if it was the scheduled flight, but for sure it had seen their signal on the beach, since it dipped its wings.

Good! The pilot would radio ahead, and Uncle Norbert would soon be heading this way.

But maybe not soon enough for Jaz. Colly's body was screaming at him to give up, but he knew he couldn't. The pressure of holding the sail against the power of the wind was wearing him down. Even though he was in good shape, windsurfing used muscles he never knew he had!

His mind was whirling as he tried to focus on which way he should be leaning. Mostly he remembered right, but once or twice or ten times, he was sure he was going to collapse. But he didn't.

He blinked back wind and spray and cheered out loud. There it was! The barge! He was directly behind it.

Watchful of men who might look back from the tug, he eased the windsurfer so that he was running alongside the barge. He angled closer, hoping to cut through the wake. Unfortunately, he'd picked the wrong side of the barge: it blocked the wind, and his sail flapped uselessly. With all the strength he had left, he threw himself toward a rope that was laced along the side of the barge. He had it! But only barely. The windsurfing board dropped away into the sea behind the barge as he clung to the side. His muscles burned with the strain of hanging on.

He moved one hand, trying for a better grip, and then the other. Just before he slipped and fell into the sea, he felt a hand on his. Jaz! He'd come to save her, and here she was saving him. It was just like her.

"Help me up!" he gasped.

Two hands reached and grabbed hold of his wrists, and before he could blink he was pulled up and over the side of the barge. Chest heaving, he reached for Jaz to hug her…and felt the slick rubber of a wet suit.

He blinked and looked up.

It was Philip!

Chapter Fifteen

"Where the heck did you come from?" Philip asked.

Colly stared at him, mouth open. Had his heart stopped beating? For a minute, he couldn't remember how to breathe.

"Where's your boat?" Philip peered over the edge of the barge. Not seeing anything, he turned back to Colly, looking more suspicious than concerned. "You'd better tell me," he said.

"I, uh…"

"You can't be a stowaway. I would have seen you."

"No!" Colly cried, wincing as Philip gripped him harder. "I was fishing, but my boat sprang a leak. When you came right up beside me I thought you saw me, but when you didn't stop, I jumped and…"

"Where is it?" Philip interrupted, his eyes narrowing.

"What?"

"Your boat."

Colly gulped. "It must have sunk." He cupped his hands over his eyes and looked behind the barge, as if searching. Relief washed through him as Philip let him go, brushing his shoulders as if trying to wipe away the pain he'd caused with his hard grip. Philip sighed and sat down on a box. He patted the box beside him, inviting Colly to sit too.

"It's okay," Colly said. "I feel like standing."

Philip shrugged. "I'm sorry it's come to this," he said.

It was a good thing their picnic by the pingo had been so many hours earlier, because Colly was sure that if he'd had anything left in his stomach, he would have puked. "Sorry for what?" he asked, pretty sure he wouldn't like the answer.

"There is no boat, Colly. You and I both know that. The only possible explanation is that you climbed on when we stopped at the pingo. Were you with Harvey? I didn't see you. I'm guessing you were with Tommy for a while, but when I grabbed him and his boat, you stayed with Harvey." Colly swallowed. There was no point in trying another lie. Philip wouldn't believe him.

"I'll bet you were listening when I was talking to Harvey back there. What I don't get is why you would come after me. They're just a bunch of stupid birds."

"But what you're doing is illegal."

Slowly, Philip nodded his head. "Ahhh…so it's because you're a Ranger?"

"I'm not a Ranger, my uncle is."

"Sure, but you're a *Junior* Ranger, and I'll bet you feel the same way he does about this sort of thing."

"Okay, you're right," Colly blurted. "I don't know what I was thinking. Just let me off on an island somewhere. By the time I get back you'll be long gone…and I won't say anything."

Philip sucked in one cheek, before speaking. "Don't try and tell me you'll keep your mouth shut."

Colly swallowed. "I will."

Philip gave an unpleasant laugh. "Don't Rangers and Junior Canadian Rangers have some sort of code of honor? I'm guessing that code doesn't include keeping any promise to me. I'm guessing the birds are more important to you."

Colly looked to his feet, and then snuck a quick glance toward the spaces in between the boxes stacked on the barge. In his head he was screaming for Jaz to stay hidden.

Philip followed his look. "What are you looking for?"

Colly inhaled sharply, silently cursing himself. "Nothing," he said. "Just looking."

Philip stood, peering at the boxes.

He had to distract him—he couldn't let him find Jaz! "Wait!" Colly cried. "What about you?"

"What about me?" Philip said, slowly turning back toward him, his gaze lingering on the stacked boxes.

"You're a wind researcher. That means you care about the environment, which should mean that you care about wild animals. Why are you taking these birds, when you know they might die?"

Philip shrugged. "Money," he said.

Colly tried to think. How much time had passed from the time that the plane had flown overhead back at the pingo? It must be a good fifteen minutes. Hopefully rescue boats were still in the water because of the town's emergency drill.

"*Just* money?" he asked, hoping Philip was feeling chatty. If he could keep him talking for a little longer, maybe they still had a chance. "Money doesn't last. There must be more to it than that."

Philip was smiling. "Now how in the heck did you know that?" he asked, looking pleased. "It's true, I have another reason."

"What is it?"

"Twenty years ago my father did the very same thing."

"In Tuk?"

"Not Tuk, no, but other places. He was part of a worldwide smuggling ring. They captured sport birds from all over North America and sold them overseas. Unfortunately, an international task force caught wind of it, and they had to stop."

"Did he go to jail?"

Philip sighed. "No, not him. He left me and my mom in California and went to work for a Saudi prince. He kept in touch, though."

"Did he tell you what to do?"

Philip grinned. "He doesn't know. This is my gift to him. My mom died five years ago, and I figured it was time to get to know dear old Dad."

"So you'll both be hanging out with Saudi royalty?"

Philip looked sharply at him. "Enough," he said. "As I'm sure you can guess, there is a lot of money involved in this. Too much to risk losing."

"Wh-what do you mean?"

Philip stood, and grabbed hold of Colly by the neck of his T-shirt. "On your feet," he said, gruffly. Philip had seemed calm, even pleased, when talking about his plan. Now he looked like a different person, mean and unpredictable.

A low rumble sounded in the distance from somewhere behind him. Philip looked over Colly's head. "Someone looking for you?" he asked.

Colly glanced up and saw the big gray body of a military Hercules aircraft. A search plane! Perhaps it had been involved in the fake rescue.

Now he could hear the high-pitched buzz of motorboats. It must be his uncle and the others, coming from town!

"I think we might just keep you around after all," Philip muttered. He grabbed Colly's shoulder and twisted him so that he was facing forward, then cranked his arm so that it would hurt if he tried to get away. "I might need a hostage."

Colly realized that Philip didn't know the boats were headed for the pingo where Harvey and Tommy had signaled the plane. He probably thought they were after him!

"No!" Colly cried, twisting and trying to get away. If only there were some way he could get his uncle's attention! He dropped to his knees, not wanting Philip to drag him out of sight. Suddenly he heard the tug's engine ease.

"What the…?" Philip cried.

Colly twisted his head around and saw fluttering white, everywhere. It was the gyrfalcons! Jaz must have set them free.

Philip was so shocked, he released his grip on Colly's arm and shoulder.

Colly rolled out of the way as the giant birds swooped around the barge, rose skyward, and seemed to drop before rising again. Colly wasn't sure if it was on purpose or an accident, but one of the birds gave Philip a glancing blow as it dropped; he lost his balance and fell off the side of the barge into the freezing water.

The RCMP search boats must have wondered about the birds, because they veered and turned toward the barge. A moment later, all but one boat was speeding toward the tug. The one that fell behind stopped to pick up Philip.

Jaz plunked herself down on the deck beside Colly.

"You're safe!" Colly cried.

Jaz cocked her head to the side and grinned. "I was starting to feel a bit bird-brained in there. It's about time you showed up!"

Chapter Sixteen

Twenty-four hours later, most of the dust had settled—
for now, anyway. Besides the local RCMP, some
important-looking men in gray suits had flown in
to interview them one at a time—Jaz, Tommy, Colly,
Harvey and Philip. The men were part of a multi-
national police force dedicated to stopping the illegal
smuggling of raptors, which was another name for birds
of prey—like gyrfalcons. That morning they flew away
again, taking Philip and the crew of the tug with them.

Uncle Norbert had said there would probably be
more interviews, but that for now they should just
enjoy the rest of their holiday.

Before their adventures, Tommy had promised to
show Colly and Jaz the town's underground storage

spaces. He met them the next afternoon at the wooden icehouse. He was carrying a key and a lantern. After glancing over his shoulder to make sure no one was looking, he unlocked the door.

"Are we sneaking in?" Jaz asked. "Will we get in trouble?"

Tommy grinned. "Nah, we're good. I just want to make sure no little kids follow us in."

"Doesn't look very big," Jaz said as they stepped inside the small space.

"And it doesn't look like a community freezer," Colly added.

"Once upon a time hunters stored meat in pingos," Tommy said. "But now they use this place. He lifted a wooden lid in the center of the floor.

Colly let out a long low whistle. "Looks like a mine shaft or something."

"At the bottom of this ladder there are three hall-ways and lots of rooms," Tommy explained.

"Can we see?" Jaz asked.

Tommy went first, and one by one they lowered themselves down the ladder.

"Watch your step," Tommy called. "The rungs can be icy."

As they climbed down, Colly noticed that at first the ground was kind of twiggy-looking and musty-smelling. Before long, though, it was solid ice, and Colly could see his breath. By the time they reached the bottom, he was shivering.

"Cool!" Jaz cried, her eyes wide.

Colly agreed. They'd entered an underground ice world. In the glow of Tommy's lantern he could see that there were wooden doors lining each hall off the open area where they stood. The walls looked like marble—or like smooth sides of an iced layer cake. The ceiling was made of a thick layer of frost gone mad. It looked as if someone had taken a bucket filled with millions of tiny diamonds and flung them upward.

"This is like some sort of cool clubhouse where superheroes come and figure out how to fix the world," Jaz said, a puff of vapor rising from her mouth.

Tommy grinned. "If you were a superhero, what would you fix?"

"I'd start with poachers," Colly said.

"Now you're talking!" Jaz cried, grinning. "Maybe we'll be super-JCRs, busting up crime rings all over the North!" She turned to Tommy, "We do have experience. Don't you agree?"

"I agree!"

"The second thing I'd fix is whatever's bugging Colly," Jaz said.

Colly frowned as both Tommy and Jaz turned to him.

"You mean he isn't always like this?" Tommy joked.

"What are you talking about?" Colly muttered, trying to swallow his annoyance.

"Actually, yeah, he's always like this. But I happen to know for a fact that he's madder than usual."

Tommy turned to him again. "What's up, bro? Anything your fellow superheroes can help with?"

"No," Colly said. He sighed. "I can handle it."

"Is it the curse?" Jaz asked.

"Jaz!"

"What? Is it a secret?"

Colly sighed again. "No, I guess not."

Jaz leaned toward Tommy. "Boys with blue eyes in his family die young and tragically," she said.

"True?" Tommy asked.

Colly nodded. "Yeah."

"And that's why you've been so touchy," Jaz said. "You always say you're not superstitious, but you are."

"Some people say being superstitious is just being careful," Tommy said. "But I think that's a joke."

Colly thought for a moment. "Maybe Jaz is right."

"Thank you!" she said, looking smug. "About what?"

"I think I *have* been superstitious about the curse, and that's making me feel different about stuff. I don't want to be worried, or scared, or any of that...but I guess I am."

Jaz grabbed him by the shoulders and gave him a shake. "Well then, don't be, Colly. All you have to do is figure it out."

"It's family history, Jaz. No mystery there."

"No? Well, maybe the problem is the way you're thinking about it. Okay, I know about your cousin. Who else had blue eyes and died?"

"Lots of people...my grandpa."

"What happened to him?"

Colly looked to the ice-crystal ceiling, remembering. "All I know is that it was New Year's Eve, and the whole family was together for dinner and games," he said. "Grandpa went to the outhouse behind our cabin. Then it was midnight, and everyone started dancing and cheering. It was a while before anyone noticed he hadn't come back in."

"Where was he?"

"He froze to death sitting on the pot." He shot Jaz a look. "Don't even think about laughing!"

"I wouldn't!" she cried as if offended. "How old was he?"

Colly shrugged. "I don't know. Fifty, maybe?"

"Who else?" Tommy asked.

Colly started ticking relatives off on his fingers. "Boating accident, froze to death, infected finger from a fishing accident…I don't know what else."

"And how old were they?"

"I'd have to ask," Colly said. "But I remember my great-auntie saying they died young."

"People always say that when people don't die of old age," Jaz said.

"That's true," Tommy agreed, nodding. "I guess if you're seventy-five, dying at fifty is dying young."

"What about blue-eyed boys who didn't die young, Colly?" Jaz asked.

He frowned. "I think there were some, but I'm not sure."

"You should check it out, man," Tommy said. "Make a list or something."

Slowly Colly nodded, feeling a weight slowly lift. "That's a good idea, Tommy. I don't know why I didn't think of that."

"You probably weren't thinking too straight after your cousin died," Jaz said gently.

"No," Colly agreed, "but I am thinking now. And what Harvey said when we were at the pingo makes sense—we can only look after what's right here, right now. I can't control what *might* happen someday. No one can."

Tommy grinned and gave him a friendly shove. Colly promised himself he would talk to his dad when he got home. One of those good long talks they didn't have often enough. They would talk about family and superstition, and he would figure things out—like Jaz said. He also needed time to grieve his cousin. He would probably never know why Junie wasn't wearing his life jacket, but he did understand it was just an accident: a stupid tragic accident. It was sad, but those kinds of things happened to lots of families, and they didn't have anything to do with curses.

There was something else. Like Harvey said, he would respect his fear and try to understand it.

He wouldn't let it control the choices he made. Most important, he wouldn't let it *change* him.

"You know what *I* think?" Jaz asked.

"What?" Colly and Tommy said together.

"I think my brain is freezing! Can we finish our save-the-world plans upstairs?"

As they emerged from the icehouse, Colly stared up at the clear blue sky. The wind had eased, and the sun was circling high in the sky around the northern pole. It would keep circling, around and around, all summer long, dipping lower and lower with each circle until it was winter, and the tundra prepared to sleep.

Even with the light, he would sleep well tonight. After all, he and his friends had been busy saving the world. They'd foiled a black-market poaching ring with roots reaching all the way to the Middle East!

A squawk made them turn. It was Beastie. He waddled toward them for a few steps, then flew to the roof of the icehouse.

"Do you still hate that bird?" Colly asked Tommy.

"Nah, he's okay."

"Good, because he and I have a lot in common, you know."

"You both have blue eyes," Jaz said. "But it's more than that."

"What?" Colly asked warily. He didn't think Jaz would call him a freak, but…

"He looks ready for anything."

Colly grinned and bumped shoulders with her. She was right. He didn't know what would happen next, but he was going to try hard not to worry about it. For sure he wouldn't let his fears stop him from doing the things that were important to him.

But, just like the bird, he would have his eyes wide open.

Blue-eyed and watchful.

"*Vigilans!*"

Anita Daher's writing reflects the places she's been blessed to spend time. Earlier Orca thrillers for young readers are *Flight from Big Tangle*, *Flight from Bear Canyon* and *Racing for Diamonds*. Anita lives in Winnipeg, Manitoba, with her family, an always-hungry basset hound and two saucy young horses.